000 / 00 2137725

SPECIAL MESSAGE TO READERS

This book is published under the auspices of
THE ULVERSCROFT FOUNDATION
(registered charity No. 264873 UK)

Established in 1972 to provide funds for
research, diagnosis and treatment of eye diseases.
Examples of contributions made are: —

A new Children's Assessment Unit at
Moorfield's Hospital, London.

•

Twin operating theatres at the
Western Ophthalmic Hospital, London.

•

A Chair of Ophthalmology at the
University of Leicester.

•

The establishment of a Royal Australian College
of Ophthalmologists "Fellowship".

You can help further the work of the Foundation
by making a donation or leaving a legacy. Every
contribution, no matter how small, is received
with gratitude. Please write for details to:

**THE ULVERSCROFT FOUNDATION,
The Green, Bradgate Road, Anstey,
Leicester LE7 7FU, England.
Telephone: (0116) 236 4325**

**In Australia write to:
THE ULVERSCROFT FOUNDATION,
c/o The Royal Australian College of
Ophthalmologists,
27, Commonwealth Street, Sydney,
N.S.W. 2010.**

THE WAY OF THE HEART

It was the scandal of the season when world-famous actress Andrea Lawrence stalked out of a Broadway hit to go home again. Home to her sister, Barbara, who would share everything with her — from her warm hospitality to handsome Hugh Robards. But the glittering, golden-haired Andrea hadn't jeopardized her career for nothing. The beautiful star was onstage for the play of her life — a drama of double-dealing romance starring her sister's fiancé.

REBECCA MARSH

THE WAY OF THE HEART

Complete and Unabridged

LINFORD
Leicester

First published in Great Britain in 1976

First Linford Edition
published 1997

Copyright © 1944, 1965 by Arcadia House
All rights reserved

British Library CIP Data

Marsh, Rebecca
 The way of the heart.—Large print ed.—
 Linford romance library
 1. English fiction—20th century
 2. Large type books
 I. Title
 823.9'14 [F]

ISBN 0–7089–5039–6

Published by
F. A. Thorpe (Publishing) Ltd.
Anstey, Leicestershire

Set by Words & Graphics Ltd.
Anstey, Leicestershire
Printed and bound in Great Britain by
T. J. Press (Padstow) Ltd., Padstow, Cornwall

This book is printed on acid-free paper

1

TAD OTT, sixteen, was hosing the red brick sidewalk in front of the Holman Variety Store on Central Street when Barbara Holman turned her Ford sedan into the six-car parking lot. Tad shut off the hose and came running to open the car door. Lest his motives be misunderstood, Tad said: "Free of charge, Miss Holman. Not that I don't want a job, because I do, but this here service is free of charge."

"Thanks, Tad."

"It's sort of like advertising, Miss Holman. See? It's just like advertising what you've got for sale in the store. Do you get the idea, Miss Holman?"

"I think I understand, Tad."

"Not that I want to hurry you, Miss Holman, but when do I go to work?"

Barbara got from the car. Tad offered

his arm and stared her into accepting its dubious support. Quite as if he were aiding an elderly lady, Tad said, "I would be careful, Miss Holman, was I you. It's a funny thing about bricks as smooth as those. They sure get slippery when they're wet."

Master Ott, Barbara noticed, had scrubbed and hosed each brick into pristine cleanliness. But he had also, she noticed, done a thorough job of messing up the windows and facade of the store. She wondered how in the world he'd gotten as much water onto the building as on the sidewalk and road.

"I don't know," she told him carefully, "that I need another boy. What work would you do? Sometimes I haven't enough work for Charles."

"Say I work ten cents an hour cheaper than Charles did, Miss Holman? Could you afford not to hire me?"

"Cheaper than Charles *did*? How come the past tense?"

Tad startled her. Flushing, scraping

a foot around and around in clockwise fashion, Tad said, "I guess Charles is in jail, Miss Holman. Not that they'll keep him there, him being a minor and all. I guess what they'll do is put him in Juvenile Hall."

Barbara unlocked the door and flicked on the ceiling lights. She left the door open so that the river breeze could rid the place of its musty smell. She waved Tad to a chair in her small office at the rear. She found Constable Allard's telephone number and dialed. During the long, long wait for an answer, she studied Master Tad Ott's face. The face had a fresh, open, merry quality she liked. Drat such faces, she thought, laughing to herself; they were created for the ultimate purpose of giving far too many women far too many emotional problems. Down with boy babies and boy-boys and boy-men!

"This here is Constable Allard speaking," a voice said in her ear.

"Hi, Norm," Barbara said. "What's

all this I hear about Charles?"

"Is this Miss Holman? Miss Holman, is that you?"

"Norm, if you've put Charles into jail, I'll not speak to you for a year! The very idea!"

"Juvenile Hall, over in Goldsborough."

"It's the same thing!"

"Now don't get fussed up, Miss Holman. With all that scandal in your very own family, you can't afford to get fussed about Charles."

"There's *no* scandal in my family. Anyway, Charles works for me, so I must look after him."

"Didn't I hear on the radio and television about your sister? Boy, she must be crazy! One guy said she was earning a hundred thousand dollars a year just for play-acting in that there musical play on Broadway."

Barbara counted to ten very slowly, and then she asked: "Must I hire a lawyer, Norm, to get the information I want about Charles?"

"Now don't you threaten me, Miss

Holman! If there's one thing I can't stand, it's a threat."

But, presently, he told her a story guaranteed to make any woman's blood run cold.

Imagine, he told her, a night dark as pitch, with owls hooting everywhere but with the river as quiet as the dead. Imagine, he went on, ten boats loaded with nine men each placed here and there on the river to corner the no-good poacher who'd been tonging all the oyster beds lately and wrecking those beds pretty thoroughly in the process. And also imagine, he elaborated, each of those men armed with a shotgun and a knife and a boat hook.

"Say," Constable Allard said conversationally, "you know what one guy planned to do with his boat hook?"

"I don't want to," Barbara said, shuddering.

"What he was gonna do, Miss Holman, was hook that no-good poacher in the stomach and then haul him around in the water until he drowned."

Barbara swallowed.

"Well, sir," Constable Allard went on, "it was very lucky for the town of Sather on the Eastern Shore of Maryland that it had Mrs. Allard's little boy Norm on the payroll and behind a badge. What Mrs. Allard's little boy Norm had done was wait on the river, too, but in a very fast cruiser equipped with a spotlight. All of a sudden he'd heard a boat, its motor throttled to low, making its way close in toward the shore to Throgg's Cove. Before anyone else could react, he'd switched on the spotlight and highballed to the poacher's boat before young Charles and his father could deep-six all those oysters they'd poached.

"Man," Constable Allard finished his tale, "I guess I prevented a massacre. All them fishermen and oysterers were howling for blood!"

"I see."

"Now about your crazy sister, Miss Holman: I been getting some calls from Baltimore and other places about her.

Reporters, mostly. They got the idea she'll show up here."

"So?"

"So what one reporter told me is that this is the big Broadway story of the year, Miss Holman. They're sure not gonna let you and your sister live in peace on that houseboat of yours."

"I demand police protection!"

"Well, I sure thank you for calling, Miss Holman, and telling me what I need to know."

"Norm, don't hang up! Please don't! What can I do to help Charles?"

For five or ten seconds he just made heavy breathing sounds. "Well," he finally answered, "I guess there's nothing much anybody can do now, Miss Holman. If there was, wouldn't I be doing it? You know how I feel about kids. But my God, Miss Holman, poaching oysters in these parts is as bad as rustling cattle in Texas. I mean, Charles and his father are up the creek."

"I'll hire a lawyer!"

Disturbed, Barbara turned from the telephone. She found the China blue eyes of Master Tad Ott studying her as they might study some odd form of insect life. She said quickly, heatedly: "Don't talk yourself out of a job, young man. Don't you dare say one word against Charles. Just scoot out and clean the front of this store as well as you cleaned the sidewalk."

"Miss Holman?"

"Scoot."

"Miss Holman?"

"Well?"

"Was I you, Miss Holman, I wouldn't waste my quarters on them. Reason I knew about this job opening up is that I was on my dad's boat last night. They sure had oysters, them Snivelys."

"And you saw where they got them, I suppose?"

"Miss Holman, they didn't get out through the Sather River channel. So they got them on the river. So they don't own any oyster beds, see?"

Barbara saw it all only too clearly.

You didn't tong up oysters from just any section of the Sather River. To tong up oysters from the Sather River, you had to go to the Kinney beds or the Northcott beds or the Oystermen's Association beds. That was it, period. And if the Snivelys hadn't left the Sather River, that was it, too, period.

The telephone rang. The operator said cheerfully that she had a long-distance telephone call for Miss Barbara Holman. Barbara waved Tad out and then told the operator she'd have to have the name of the caller. The gravelly voice of Simon Levine broke in to say, "Look, doll baby, on you coyness isn't becoming."

Barbara took the call resignedly. "But I don't adore you, Mr. Levine," she reported. "I thought an agent's supposed to keep a star out of trouble."

"Is she there?"

"No."

"Has she telephoned?"

"No."

"If you ask me, she's flipped! What

happened last night was that Mark Banes said she was throwing in too many ad libs and that the authors of the play were complaining. Your sister blew higher than Old Faithful geyser. Before anybody knew it, she was gone, and the curtain was rising for the second act."

Barbara sighed. "That's Andy," she reported. "She used to have tantrums right in our living room if anyone broke up what she used to call her performance mood. I'm surprised the director criticized her during a performance."

"Well, that wasn't smart," Mr. Levine conceded, "and I chewed his ear off for being so stupid. But that's water under the bridge. The star is gone! Everything's in an uproar here! We announced Andrea's understudy for tonight, and did we get cancellations!"

"If I see her, I'll scold her, how's that?"

"Sure. Now don't talk to the press, catch? The last thing we want now is a loudmouth speaking the wrong lines."

"I insist I'm not a loudmouth, Mr. Levine. But I'll give no interviews. Why should I? It's Andy's career and loot; not mine."

"She has to be nuts! A hundred grand a year — and Hollywood and television waving at her with more money bags! So what does she do?"

Still sputtering, Mr. Levine broke the connection, presumably to go find an aspirin.

Barbara wasted no mental energy on that problem, however. She checked her desk clock and then went out to the street. She locked the door and told young Tad Ott that she'd not be long, and then she headed across the road to the cute board-and-batten building housing the law offices of Peter Jay Nock. Peter was dictating something or other to his secretary in the reception room, but he broke off and rose grinningly. "I suspected you'd be here early," Peter said. "That's why I'm early."

He showed her into his office and seated her. Hazel eyes grim, he went behind the desk, there to shake his head. "Candidly," he told her, "father and son don't have a chance. I'll take the case, if you insist, but I have to tell you the money will be wasted."

"Peter, the boy worked for me. He was a quite good worker, perfectly trustworthy and dependable. I can't just abandon him."

"I doubted you would, which also explains why I'm here early. I may as well tell you that I stopped at the constable's office before I came. We had a good talk. On the evidence, the best any lawyer can do is plead mitigating circumstances for the boy and throw him on the mercy of the court."

"Peter, how in the world is it possible for a nice boy like Charles to become involved in such a thing?"

"Maybe the father gave orders, and the boy was afraid to disobey. Who knows? I'll check into all that if you want to waste your money."

Barbara had to ask self-consciously: "How much money's involved, Peter? I'm not overloaded with cash just now, because I've had to restock my store for the spring and summer trade."

"What about paying me with a kiss?"

"Peter, this is *not* the time for nonsense."

"Sure. You adore Hugh Robards and intend to marry him. Also, you have Andy on your mind and Charles on your mind. But do you know what? To me, it wouldn't be nonsense."

"I'll pay up to a thousand dollars."

He studied her lovely face, her troubled brown eyes, and sighed. "Well, okay," he agreed. "But I wish you were Andy. Andy was too practical, wasn't she, to remain involved with Hugh Robards?"

Barbara forgave him the crack, figuring that a kind fellow ought to be done a kindness once in a while. Elated, she went back to the store and opened for the day.

2

ABOARD the *River Lark* on Wednesday evening, Hugh Robards switched off the television set and pulled a cigar from his pocket and lighted up. Looking at nothing in particular through the salon window, Hugh said in musing tones, "It's all darned strange, don't you think? Of course, everything about Andy has always been darned strange. I remember seeing her one evening on Sather Pier. The wind was blowing practically at gale force, and the water was running high. There Andy stood in her floppy-tailed shirt and dungarees, her arms spread as wide as possible, her head flung back, her golden hair streaming loose and very beautiful. Suddenly she began to dance like one of those ballerinas you see on television. She didn't seem to need any music. Around and around she went, so lightly and prettily that it grabbed me. In a strange way, she was a girl I'd never seen before. Yet she was just Andy Lawrence, your half-sister, a fifteen-year-old small-town kid. I saw that easily enough when she stopped dancing all alone at the end of the pier."

"More coffee, Hugh?"

"Well, perhaps a drop more. That was quite a dinner."

"You say that every Wednesday evening."

"I do?"

"Yes. You always say, 'Well, perhaps a drop more. That was quite a dinner.' It's interesting."

"Girls notice the strangest things."

"Possibly a girl might think it strange that a rough and tough hero man stopped to watch a dancer on a pier one evening."

A tall muscular man with quiet, rather placid gray eyes, Hugh went to the counter between the salon and galley to have a drop more coffee poured into his cup. He did a rare thing. As Barbara leaned forward to pour, he kissed the tip of her nose. Hugh said, his voice furry with emotion, "Don't ever change much as we grow old together. All right? I happen to like you as you are."

They went out to the wicker chairs on the starboard deck. They found the sunset coming along beautifully: half the sky was a glowing red speckled with very bright golds; all the open water of Sather Creek was a softer red shading into purple; all the trees across the creek were outlined sharply by the backlight. To Barbara, the most interesting thing about this particular sunset hour was the unusual hush. She could neither see nor hear a bird anywhere, and the water spread before them was as still and quiet as glass. A girl could do far worse, she thought, than live in a houseboat on Sather Creek.

Hugh said again, "Yes, it's all

darned strange, don't you think? Andy was almost childishly proud of the reviews she got for her opening night performance. Did I ever tell you she sent me a flock of those reviews?"

"Really?"

"Also, one of the publicity pictures, a large glossy thing showing her in one of her costumes. In the letter she included, Andy said she hoped to play Daisy in *I Found A Daisy* for at least two years. Now this!"

Troubled, Barbara had to say, "I didn't know she kept in touch with you."

"Between you and me, Barbara, there's a lonely girl. That's natural, I guess. I've read somewhere that richly talented people are always lonely people. Their talent, the writer said, separates them from average people. The writer said that their talent puts them way up there like a mountain peak. I've never thought of a mountain peak as being lonely, have you?"

"I've never thought of Andy as

being lonely. Her letters are always gay, always filled with chatter about lively parties and interesting people."

Hugh knocked ash from the cigar. "I guess," he said, "Andy writes me occasionally for reasons other than loneliness. For instance, on that picture she sent me she wrote: 'Here I am; where are you?' I guess she needs to impress someone she knew when she was just a fifteen-year-old girl in a floppy-tailed shirt and dungarees."

Barbara tightened her lips to make sure she'd not say a word. She found an odd comfort in fingering her engagement ring. Or was it so odd that the ring comforted her? This much she had, and was there anything to surpass it?

Hugh asked, surprising her: "This upcoming marriage of ours — you don't suppose it's upset Andy, do you?"

"What? But why?"

"She's so strange, you see. Let me tell you something I've not told you before. I put Andy aboard the train in Easton the morning she headed for New York City. She was all nerves. She wanted to try for a career, but she also wanted to stay in Sather and — well, and marry me, as you know. But she had to have her dream. That's what she babbled as I drove her to Easton. She babbled it over and over again, as if she were trying to sell herself that what she was doing was right. Well, the thing I wanted to tell you is that I could have stopped Andy that day."

"No."

"Yes."

"Because, you see," Barbara told him, "Andy and I sat up half the night talking before you came in your car. We talked mostly about a very complex subject called true feminine fulfillment. For Andy, it could be achieved only through a glittering career. She was sorry about that, genuinely sorry, but she wouldn't have stayed had you asked her to marry you then and there."

"Really?"

"Really."

Hugh tossed his cigar overboard, smiling broadly and squaring his shoulders. "I'm glad to hear that," he said. "I've felt guilty, I don't mind telling you."

His hand came toward Barbara's, and she allowed it to find hers on her lap. Now she did hear and see a bird, a fiercelooking kingfisher driving hard across the sunset flame toward Throgg's Cove in the distance. She loved the raffish appearance of the bird. Silly though the thought was, she was glad suddenly that the bird was so free. But then she heard more in the sunset quiet, the dull chunk-chunk-chunk of the elderly fantail fishing boat Hugh had sold her father at cost. She went down to the stern deck to smile and wave encouragingly as the landlubber worked the boat around trot-line floats and moored craft preliminary to tying up alongside the *River Lark*. This evening her father did quite well. There were only two near-accidents, and her father came alongside with minimal wear and tear on anyone's nerves. Hugh caught the line tossed up to the port deck and snubbed it around a bitt. He leaned over the rope rail to give her father a hand up. Naturally, Vincent Holman spurned the proffered hand. "Son," he drawled, "you should see me scrambling around a scaffold when I'm putting up a big building. What I have in my veins is monkey blood."

Short, sturdy, his brown eyes twinkling, he came aboard and gave Barbara a paternal swat on the back of her plaid skirt. "Your mother's going nuts," Mr. Holman confided. "She tells me to turn off the radio, so I do. Then she asks why I turned the radio off; am I trying to keep something from her? Hugh, let me tell you something about women you've maybe missed. Look at any woman and you look at a great big mystery."

"Lovely mysteries, Vince, don't you think?"

"That's the truth! Here I've been married to a woman all these years, and I've fathered a woman and I've helped to raise two women, yet every time I look at any of them I'm plain puzzled. What makes them tick? Go ahead and tell me!"

Instead, Hugh looked at his watch and said he'd have to get back to his boat yard. Barbara made the customary protest, but Hugh was as deaf as ever when work was involved. "The Conlogues are coming Saturday," he explained, "and I promised their schooner would be in the water. I've got to get a new mast stepped in."

Barbara was given a placatory kiss. It didn't quite placate her, but Hugh went off anyway along the pier to the land. He beeped three times, as usual, before he drove away in his green pickup truck.

"Nice tactful guy," Mr. Holman said approvingly when the sound of the truck motor had died away. "I guess he'll make a nice addition to the family.

Your mother was saying the same thing just yesterday."

"Glad you approve, Dad. Want cognac in your coffee?"

"Why else would I come here? To me, a houseboat isn't a home. To me, frankly, a houseboat is an insult to every carpenter who ever pounded a nail."

Grinning, Barbara took him into the salon, warmed the coffee, added a jigger of cognac, and served him with a proper curtsey. "It so happens," she said, "that a carpenter built the *River Lark*. It so happens that Hugh employs three bona fide carpenters in the boat yard."

"To me, a home isn't a home unless there's solid land under it. Maybe I'm old-fashioned, but I'd rather have a front yard with gophers in it than minnows and jellyfish."

"You're old-fashioned," Barbara assured him.

Her father sipped the drink and sighed. He looked tired and sunburned and worried. "Good," he pronounced it. "That's quite a job I'm on right now. This lady whose home I'm building changes her mind about things almost as fast as I nail a stud into place. I keep telling her that changes cost money, big money, but not even that stops her from making changes. Yet she's not rich. That worries me, because the guys have to be paid when they redo things, and the changes sure aren't worth all the extra money they're costing her."

"Maybe I'd better talk to her."

"Some people you can't talk to, and that's a fact. Like Andy, I guess."

Barbara smiled faintly, glad he'd come to the point of his visit at last. "How many telephone calls have you and Mom had? I've had several dozen."

"Edna's pretty upset, honey."

"She shouldn't be," Barbara said quickly. "Dad, that half-sister of mine is a pretty resourceful character. The one thing none of us should do is worry about her."

"Edna has a notion that Andy's scared she's losing something big." Mr. Holman took another sip of the coffee and cognac. "Meaning Hugh," he explained. "I guess your mother figures Andy won't ever get Hugh out of her system."

The idea made Barbara uncomfortable. She sat near the imitation-brick fireplace and looked moodily at the brass andirons. The andirons needed polishing, she saw. In fact, she thought, the *River Lark* was long overdue for its annual spring cleanup. She wondered if Master Tad Ott would consider such work beneath him. Charles Snively never had, but no two boys were ever quite the same.

"I don't understand Andy," Mr. Holman said glumly. "That figures, her already being on the scene a few years when I married Edna. Sometimes I think I don't really know Andy even a little bit."

"You're her favorite father — so she's told me."

"It's funny, but I've always felt like I am her father. Still, I don't understand her like I do you. I — well, look, honey, why don't I stop making conversation and just say what I came to say? I think you and Hugh should move your wedding day from June fifteenth to — well, tomorrow."

Puzzled, Barbara looked up from the andirons.

"Maybe I'm crazy," Mr. Holman said, "but I think doing that would be a real smart idea. After all, Hugh is a guy, and you know how guys are. I don't care how noble a guy is, he can be worked on by any woman who wants to work on him. Andy's not just any woman, either. Andy's a beautiful blonde, earning big money and becoming more and more famous and glamorous every week. Also, she knows Hugh Robards pretty well. If Andy comes here to work on Hugh — "

"Now, now, now."

"It could be. Your mother thinks so,

too. We want you to be happy, too, you know."

"Grab a husband tomorrow for fear I can't keep him if I'm faced with competition? If I felt I had to do such a thing, how could I be happy with the husband?"

"Well . . ."

To change the delicate subject, Barbara said abruptly, "I've hired Peter to do what he can for Charles Snively, Dad. I suppose some people will resent that, but I felt I owed the boy that much support."

Mr. Vincent Holman had views on *that* subject, too, it developed — so to Barbara's relief, the delicate subject was changed in a hurry.

"Boy," her father began, "are you ever nuts!"

3

THE recorded voice of Leonard Warren singing the *Il Balen Del Suo Sorriso* aria from *Il Trovatore* came exquisitely to Andrea Lawrence's ears as she stood powdering her freshly showered body in her penthouse apartment overlooking the Hudson River. Andrea thought wryly that far too many composers made far too much fuss about the tempests of the heart. But if one had to sing about such matters, this particular song was the one to sing. Andrea thought it a pity that a man possessed of so rich a voice as Mr. Leonard Warren had possessed should have died so relatively young. She pattered to the living room as the aria ended. She switched off the record player and put the record back into the proper album. Walking lightly, almost airily, Andrea continued on to the kitchen and poked her golden head a foot or so in through the doorway. "I'll have an omelette," she told Mrs. Rennick. "Tea would be nice for a change."

"You'll have your death of cold, too," Mrs. Rennick scolded, "if you don't stop walking around in your pelt. The idea!"

"The skin must breathe, you see. It's very important to expose your whole body to fresh air at least two hours a day."

"If you ask me, Miss Lawrence, it's more important to you right now to go back to being Daisy."

"But I didn't ask you, did I?" Andrea's sunny smile, however, prevented the question from giving offense. "I'll have the omelette on the terrace in twenty minutes. Oh, and you may as well make a big pot of coffee. Mr. Levine will be here at six, and Mr. Hogan will be here at seven. Be sure not to let any reporters in when you open up for my guests."

"Miss Lawrence, I'd like to say something I've been thinking about."

"Well?"

Mrs. Rennick stepped away from the kitchen sink. She stood with her arms loose at her sides, her shoulders squared, her head tilted a bit as if she were trying to look over the sharp glare of footlights. "I want you to take a real good look at me, Miss Lawrence," the woman said. "I want you to look at my hair and my face and my uniform and my hands. Not a lovely sight, am I?"

"Oh, dear, don't be glum again, Mrs. Rennick. I don't adore you when you're glum!"

"Once upon a time, Miss Lawrence, believe it or not, I was as lovely as you — just as slender, just as saucy, just as arrogant."

"I'm simply never arrogant any more, Mrs. Rennick. I used to be, I'll admit. But once, when I was fifteen, I made the mistake of trying to upstage my sister while we were on Sather Pier. Never annoy Barbara! That sweet, good-humored face conceals the ferocity of a tigress! That day, Barbara pushed me off the pier."

Mrs. Rennick laughed; she had to.

"But perhaps," Andrea conceded, "I do have a certain measure of conceit. A woman ought not to be conceited, I suppose, but there are so many attentive men, so many invitations, so many — "

"What I'm trying to say," Mrs. Rennick interrupted, "is that everybody once predicted I'd be a great Broadway star, too. But I flung my weight around as you're doing right now — and see what happened."

"Will you not look so glum? Will you please not? Why, you're a wonderful cook and housekeeper! What's so horrid about being that?"

"Well, it isn't being a star, you know."

"Very well. You've warned me. There! You've done your duty, so now glumness can end. Did I say I want an omelette?"

Humming, loving the cool air on her body, Andrea returned to her bedroom. She put on panties and bra. After long thought, she put on turquoise lounging slacks and a short-sleeved black cashmere sweater. She was slipping her feet into black flats when Mrs. Rennick came in with the omelette, English muffins, and tea. Mrs. Rennick arranged the snack just so on the table on the terrace. After Andrea had seated herself, Mrs. Rennick poured the tea. "Don't look now," Mrs. Rennick said, "but there's a fellow with a camera on the next roof."

"Shoot him, there's a dear."

"His angle's bad, Miss Lawrence. As long as you don't get over there near the railing, he can't shoot a picture worth printing."

Mrs. Rennick went indoors. Andrea ate quickly and heartily, concentrating on the snack until only the tea was left. She then went to the chaise longue and arranged it so that she could look at the river and distant New Jersey without craning from the pillow. Think, think, think! To hustle down to Sather, or not to?

While she was still trying to decide, Mrs. Rennick came out through the living room slide-door and announced most respectfully: "Mr. Levine, Miss Lawrence."

Simon pumped his legs vigorously to the gate of the bedroom terrace. "You kill me," he said hotly. "A great big ball of wax is going down the drain, but there you sit mooning at a river!"

"Enter," laughed Andrea, "the storm!"

"Just to make me giggle," Simon said, "tell me how you expect to pay the rent on this place. Right now, I would love to giggle."

"Want some tea?"

The agent made a gagging sound. He took the wrought-iron chair near the wrought-iron railing, sitting with his back to the view. At fifty-five, Simon Levine was a short, barrel-chested man whose dark eyes stared owlishly through black-rimmed glasses. He wore a dark gray suit, narrow-toed black shoes, a rich silk necktie. For 'color,' he wore also a diamond stickpin, diamond cuff links, and a star sapphire ring on the pinky of each hand. From a silver cigar case he extracted an enormous panatella, and he clipped it, holed it, and lighted up. He was a performance, Andrea mused. Neither the theater, nor motion pictures, nor television had anything quite compared with him.

"So what do you want?" Simon asked after he'd puffed awhile. "You want blood? I'll take you to the theater, and you can see blood. A lot of people are dying because the show's got everything but the right Daisy."

"Simon, will you not be glum? I abhor glumness."

"Tell me what great big crime Mark Banes committed. That's all I ask. Is that asking too much?"

"Simon, we've been over all this."

"The trouble is, they've got your

name on a contract. I know that an artist doesn't like to hear such dull business talk, but you'll have to listen to it either here or in court."

"Court?"

"That's a place where a judge says one day that you have to make up the losses the producers have suffered because of your walkout."

"Why should I do that?"

"Because you walked out. You have a contract calling for you to appear in *I Found A Daisy* six evenings and two matinees every week for the run of the play. You haven't been doing that lately, if I may remind you."

Andrea sipped the tea. It tried her patience to have Simon sitting in exactly the right place on the terrace to ruin the view. "I wish you'd move to the left or right," she told him. "You know I adore the view."

"I kid you not about the lawsuit, Andy."

"Have I said you may call me Andy?"

"Yes."

"How nice. I'm dreadfully fond of you, Simon, you see. I was simply nothing at all, was I, when I came to your office and said I would allow you to be my agent? But you perceived in me this interesting talent I have, and here we are. You may continue to call me Andy."

She was very lovely in that moment. Her face had charming freshness; her great blue eyes had imps in their depths. She was to him in that moment eternal girl as well as eternal woman, and when he realized this Mr. Simon Levine huffed and puffed mightily on his enormous cigar.

"I was criticized publicly by Mr. Banes," Andrea told him. "He expressed dissatisfaction with my performance. I naturally assumed that he wanted to see the last of me, so I left. I think, all things considered, that I contrived a rather dignified exit."

"He didn't specifically fire you."

"I shall wear black when I appear

in court. You might cue my lawyer to ask why I'm wearing black. Then I'll say in properly sad tones that I'm in mourning for the death of all my hopes. Then I shall raise my eyes to the face of this dear, understanding judge and confide in him that I had hoped to play Daisy for the next several years."

"You know what's wrong with you, Andy?"

"What?"

"You've been thinking. Girls always get into trouble, I find, when they start thinking."

"Well, a girl must try, mustn't she?"

"As long as it doesn't cost you and me big money, I couldn't care less. But when it costs money — stop."

"Do I look well in black, do you think?"

"Andy?"

"Simon?"

"Let the kids live. Your sister, I mean, and the boat builder. They're nice kids."

It shook Andrea Lawrence. She

snapped: "That's a mean thing to say!"

"What you're sore about," he said, unruffled, "is that you can't ever fool me with an act."

"Why in the world should I want to do anything to prevent their marriage?"

"Simple. You're not the first girl I've met, you know, who came to New York with stars in her eyes and a hick-town hero in her heart. It's always the same. The girl thinks it's okay to make the guy wait until she's had her fling on the stage. But let the guy make one move to indicate he's wiggling off the hook — then he's a no-good selfish slob."

"I think you had better leave."

"I think you'd better honor your contract."

"Mr. Banes discharged me."

"You can't prove that, Andy, and you know it."

But, as he'd accused her, she'd been thinking. "If a judge tells me, Simon, that my opinion in the matter is wrong, then I'll apologize and return to the show. It's my best judgment now, however, that my opinion isn't wrong."

"Hey!"

"I wonder how long it will take Mr. Banes and the producers to get me into court, Simon? Bruce seems to think it will take three or four months."

"Look, Andy, this could kill your career!"

"An honest mistake is no crime, Simon."

Beginning to perspire, he put the cigar out in the nearest ash tray. "All for what?" he yelled. "All for what?"

Mrs. Rennick came out, looking annoyed. "Mr. Hogan's here, Miss Lawrence," she announced. "I thought he was coming at seven."

Chuckling, Andrea hurried through the bedroom and along the main hall to the living room. This once she allowed Bruce Hogan a kiss on her forehead. "Will you not be so glum and businesslike? she begged. "Everyone's so glum and businesslike these days."

Simon Levine came pumping into the living room. "Hogan," he yelled, "talk sense into this nut before she kills her career!"

Simon Levine stopped yelling. The hard gray eyes of Bruce Hogan told him he had better, so Simon did.

4

MASTER TAD OTT said that cleaning a houseboat wasn't exactly his idea of what learning the merchandising business was all about. He went to the stern deck of the *River Lark* and stood looking at the boats moving in and out of Sather Creek. One sight was really worth looking at. A quarter-mile upstream, the Conlogues' schooner was standing out from the Hugh Robards Boat Yard. All the sails were up to catch the following breeze, and the schooner was most impressive as it glided gracefully south for its trial run on the Sather River. "Boy," Tad marveled, "imagine anybody owning a boat like her."

"You buy them with money," Barbara explained. "You earn a dollar doing this chore and a dollar doing that chore. You never turn down a chance to earn a dollar. One fine day, you have enough money to spend on luxuries. If you wish, you spend some of your money on a schooner."

Tad waved as the schooner slipped by them. Someone waved back, a fact that pleased Tad. "When I'm rich," Tad said, "I'll be just as democratic as all the rich folks that come to Sather. I won't snub anybody."

"Fine. Now, then, shall we start the cleaning?"

Tad scowled, but nodded. They spent all of Saturday morning doing the guest stateroom and bathroom. They began by washing the overhead and then the bulkheads and then the decks. While Tad busied himself polishing all the metalwork, Barbara changed the linen and curtains and saw to several repairs in the bathroom. They lunched on canned pea soup, roast beef sandwiches, and Seven-Up. After the traditional hour's wait to get the lunch settled nicely, Barbara let the boy change into the swim trunks he'd brought along and go overboard for some swimming. She watched him a while, thinking it odd that so handsome a young fellow shouldn't have at least three or four of the loveliest Sather girls in tow this beautiful late-April day. She changed into a swimsuit, thinking to give him at least some company in the water until it was time to get back to work. When she returned to the deck, though, she discovered that Tad had taken care of his own social well-being quite shrewdly. A scrappy-cat was sailing alongside the *River Lark*, four roses of the high school set squealing to Tad and waving mops and scrub brushes. Grinning, Tad clambered aboard the *River Lark*. "What I kind of thought," he explained to Barbara, "was that I'd give those dizzy dolls a break by letting them help me this afternoon. They're all in bathing suits, see? That's so they can stand in the water and scrub the keel nice and clean."

"*Sweet* of you."

"Then after some chow and dancing, maybe, I could talk them into helping us in the salon and galley. We'd get most of the work done today that way, wouldn't we?"

"Tad, I can't afford to pay each of those girls a dollar an hour. Even if I could, I wouldn't. Certain things are worth just so much and not a penny more. It isn't worth sixteen dollars extra to me to have the place cleaned this afternoon."

"Guess what, Miss Holman?"

"Well?"

"I sort of said that I sort of thought it would be pretty logical for your sister to come today. I sort of said that I sort of thought you'd maybe be glad to introduce her to folks who like you so much they'll do your housework for free."

Barbara never did get the time to answer *that*. The girls came charging aboard, four healthy, lively, noisy youngsters who said they found it tough to be aboard, and would you *see* that cute slavemaster, wheee! Tad allowed them to fuss over him for a time. Male-like, though, he never forgot the reason he'd had them come there. At two-thirty promptly, he told them to make like eager-beaver mermaids. Soon he was in the water with them, supervising their cleaning of the pale yellow keel.

Barbara changed back into dungarees and a T-shirt. She discovered that if she went without hamburger for dinner that evening, she could make two hamburger sandwiches for each youngster. The apple pie she'd been saving for dinner tomorrow evening would have to be sacrificed, too, she discovered.

The telephone interrupted the food preparations.

From far, far away, Andy said in her ear, "Hi, Britches, how are you?"

"Andy? Is that you, Andy? You goose! Andy, you silly goose!"

"Now there's a fine opening line,

Britches. Do you know where Wilmington, Delaware, is?"

"What are you doing there?"

"Simple. I'm waiting for an Easton train to come along to carry me to the Eastern Shore. I should get to Easton by six."

"I'll scoop you up!"

"Oh, I'll hire a car. How are the folks?"

"Disturbed, I'll tell you that!"

"It's their age," Andy said. "Have you noticed how dreadfully distrait parents become whenever — "

"What about the lawsuit?"

"Whoops, there's my train!"

The connection went dead, and Barbara hung up.

Tad knocked on the starboard. "They can use some cleaning powder," he reported. He hesitated, looking embarrassed, and then he said, "I sort of heard your end of the conversation, Miss Holman. I wasn't snooping. You was talking pretty loud."

"It's quite all right, Tad. I always

trust people who work for me. I suppose some would argue that's not a good idea, poor Charles Snively's plight considered. I wonder if the girls would take a rain check for that introduction to my sister? I'm sure she'll be rather tired and upset by the time she gets here."

"Sure."

Barbara found a couple of cans of scouring powder in a supply cupboard. About five minutes after Tad had gone out, all work stopped, and the chatter and laughter with it. For a time Barbara wondered if the girls were going to call off the deal they'd made with Tad, but presently the girls were working again, and the chatter and laughter went on as before. The girls worked steadily and efficiently. By three-thirty, even Tad was saying they'd done a pretty darned good job on the keel. He called for Barbara to take a look. To do a good inspection, Barbara had to put on her bathing suit and get down there in the water. The keel, she found, was immaculate. There wasn't a smudge or a barnacle anywhere to mar the smooth, lovely yellow. Delighted, she had the kids come aboard. While Tad got the record-player and dancing going, she did the sandwiches and poured the Cokes and Seven-Ups. She joined the youngsters on the bow deck, stretching out comfortably in the warm sunshine, her back to one of the rail posts. One girl, Candy Withoyt, told Tad to squelch the record-player. "Miss Holman," she asked, "how come almost everybody in town is sure that Charles is guilty and you're not so sure?"

"Are they sure?"

Another girl warned: "You better be on your guard, Miss Holman. Candy's the editor of our high school newspaper. Candy, you're being unethical! You're supposed to tell people before you interview them that you represent the press."

"I intended to."

"How do you like editing the paper under Mrs. Lucas?" Barbara asked. "I was on the staff of the *Sather High School Chatter* for a while."

"I know," Candy said. Candy sighed, a thin, flat-chested girl with a long face and rather hollow cheeks. "We can't print today the stuff you used to print, though. Mrs. Lucas insists that we print no controversial material. I'm not so sure I approve of limiting reporters that way. I mean, I think a reporter's paramount job is getting the facts and printing the facts. How can you have an informed student body if you don't give the student body complete information?"

The girl who'd criticized Candy announced gigglingly, "Candy's a born rebel, Miss Holman. I guess Candy would rather print controversial material than eat."

"Star Cuthbert, that isn't true! All I say is that if it's all right to compliment the PTA about this or that, it should be all right to criticize the PTA about this or that, too."

Tad said thoughtfully, "Well, the

school wheels are in a spot, Candy. Take modern American history. If Miss Green says anything good about Franklin Delano Roosevelt, somebody on the school board is sure to wonder if maybe Miss Green is a socialist or even a Communist. So I guess they have to play things safe."

"Then how can a person learn?" Candy asked. "I mean, if information is suppressed right in the classroom, how is a person going to learn anything much? Take social security, for example. I hear adults criticizing social security, but I never hear about adults refusing social security checks when they're due. Well, why do they disapprove of social security, and why do they take checks from a program they disapprove?"

Barbara said carefully, "I can answer your original question this way, Candy: I have no views whatsoever on the innocence or guilt of Charles Snively. In my opinion, it will be up to the judge to make the determination. I've hired Mr. Nock to represent Charles because Charles did work for me honestly and reliably and loyally, and I think he's entitled to my support now."

"Miss Holman, shouldn't your first loyalty be to law and order?" It was June Enderby who asked the question, a rather tubby miss of fifteen with cool blue eyes. "My folks think that society should come first."

Tad was indignant. "What kind of question is that?" he asked. "It says right in the books that people accused of a crime have a right to be defended by a lawyer."

There ensued twenty or so minutes of debate on the question, and then the debate was terminated by Candy Withoyt. Candy told Barbara sadly, "All the kids at the school, Miss Holman, know darned well that Charles is guilty. We know a lot more about Charles than we'll ever tell. I guess that's why we're all so interested in his case."

Tad jumped up and said crisply, "Stow it, Candy. We've got some more work to do, remember?"

But he was talking to a young lady who believed in freedom of speech. "What I think," Candy told Barbara, "is that Charles should be sent to a psychiatrist. A lot of things Charles does aren't normal, in my opinion."

"Such as?"

Star Cuthbert said, grimacing, "Like sometimes Miss Holman, Charles likes to pull a fish out of the water and just stand there watching it flop and wiggle until it dies."

Barbara drew a deep breath.

"Or you take bees," June said. "Charles likes to catch bees and pull their wings off and then make them race and fight."

Tad said grimly, "If a lot of long tongues don't stop wagging, I'm gonna cross some names off my list."

It was a revelation to see how quickly the girls stopped talking and went back to work.

By five o'clock the work was finished and the youngsters were sailing off in the scrappy-cat sailboat toward the Sather River. Disturbed by some of the statements she'd heard, Barbara telephoned Peter Jay Nock. Peter came driving over fifteen minutes later. When he learned that her sister was due in Easton at six o'clock, he volunteered to drive Barbara to meet her. "Not that I'm a kind chap," Peter said wryly, "but it's one way of being alone with you for a while."

He waited on deck until Barbara had made herself presentable. Quite as if he thought she was a novice on the catwalk, he steadied her with hands around her waist as they went along the narrow catwalk to the shore. In the car, however, he did keep both hands on the steering wheel. After they'd gotten beyond Sather limits, he slowed the car somewhat so they could enjoy the farmland scenery and talk. "About Charles," he said. "Since the fellow is a minor, he'll go before a judge in a closed trial. I imagine the judge will order all sorts of examinations — a psychiatric one included. The court isn't interested in punishing minors, but in rehabilitating them. He's an odd fellow, you know."

"That's what troubles me, Peter. I never did know. He was always quiet, polite, cheerful, helpful, dependable."

"He likes you. I suppose I should be honest and say he has a crush on you."

"Oh, my goodness!"

"According to him, you're always a great lady."

"Well, boys that age don't see much, fortunately."

"Who knows? At any rate, I agree with his high opinion of you. You'll make a fine addition to the Nock family, I'm sure."

Exasperated, Barbara asked: "Will you *not* be silly?"

A handsome, moneyed fellow, much too sure of himself to suit her, Peter

Jay Nock murmured: "The one thing I never am is silly, Barbara. As you'll learn, I'm sure, as you'll learn."

They reached Easton just as the train came in.

5

ANDY insisted upon swimming in the nude. "It's so dark," she said, "even an owl couldn't see me. And my skin has to breathe! It's important for my skin to breathe!" The next moment, Andy was overboard and splashing away contentedly in the cold water of Sather Creek. Barbara stood at the rail, watching with what seemed to her to be a much too maternal indulgence. "You're lucky," she called. "We've had no hot weather to speak of, so there aren't any jellyfish."

"It even *tastes* good!"

When Andy came back aboard, her golden hair was plastered to her head. Laughing, shivering, she grabbed a towel from Barbara's hands and draped it about herself. "I'm a squaw!" Andy cried. "Heap big fire for iced squaw!"

Still feeling maternally indulgent,

Barbara lighted a fire in the imitation-brick fireplace in the salon. She drew all the draperies and laid another towel on the floor and ordered: "All right, Miss Primitive, toast your bones. But what's this nonsense about your skin? My, the nonsense you pick up in New York."

"I have such lovely skin, did you know?"

"I've even heard it said, Andy, that you're a lovely woman. I've read that in some of the New York reviews you sent me."

"Oh, but that's another matter, quite irrelevant, really." Andy's great blue eyes twinkled in the glow of the crackling fire. "You see, most newspaper critics are elderly men and women to whom almost any young person appears to be beautiful or handsome. Smile with the proper sass at the old men or with becoming modesty at the old ladies, and they're almost sure to pay your beauty one or two graceful tributes."

"Why, you little cynic!"

Barbara went on to the galley to get their dinner started. She had a good fifteen minutes alone there in which to organize both the dinner and her thoughts. She knew now that it was no confused or overly tired or hurt Andy who'd come to the Eastern Shore. Her sister was at the peak of her beauty, surely, and she had the confidence and clear-headedness of a woman who knew it. Therefore, the newspapers hadn't yet printed the real reason Andy had just walked away from the show, her contract notwithstanding. So, of course, a girl had to give at least some thought to the possibility a pair of troubled parents had raised. But why would Andy, at this late date, throw away everything she'd achieved to fight for a fellow she could have married a few years ago just for the nodding? It didn't make sense.

Andy came into the kitchen, looking fetching and comfortable in slacks and sweater, socks and thong sandals. Andy had fluffed her hair prettily, and she'd gotten all the make-up removed. Her beauty excepted, there was nothing to distinguish her from the average Sather girl. Her clothes, while attractive, didn't look particularly expensive. In fact, Barbara thought, studying the slacks, she had a rack of slacks in her store that could compare favorably with Andy's.

"Nothing elaborate," Andy said. "An omelette would be nice."

"Nope."

"Oh?"

"Mrs. Rennick sent me a letter, Andy. She's concerned because you don't eat proper meals at proper times. She said you tend to live on omelettes and quickie snacks."

"Oh, dear, I abhor tattletales, don't you?"

Andy went around the counter and sat on one of the stools. She gazed about the salon for a while, and then she gazed about the galley. "It's a lovely home," she told Barbara. "It's not what I would have expected you to settle for, but it's a lovely home."

"What did you expect me to settle for?"

"Oh, I suppose I expected you to repeat the pattern cut by our estimable parents. A little tract of earth, a little garden, a white-frame house facing the sea, the traditional picket fence, chicken dinner every Sunday at noon — all that."

"Well, I do own a not-so-little tract of earth. I'll show you tomorrow. I have two acres along this creek, so that if a nitwit sister comes along to swim in the raw she may do so in reasonable privacy. But I enjoy living on the water. I find it restful."

"Garden?"

"Well, not here. I do have a small garden along the parking lot beside my store. I'm afraid I don't make any points for myself, though, with the ladies of the Sather Garden Club. Someone's always popping in to exhort me to do better for the sake of the town."

Andy laughed rippling, delicate

laughter. "I'm delighted to know," she said, "that Sather hasn't changed."

Barbara studied the chickens in the electric rotisserie. She thought that five minutes more ought to finish them. She mixed oil and vinegar into the salad and served. Andy pulled her wooden bowl to her eagerly and began to eat. "I do wish you could come to New York and cook for me," Andy said. "You're a much better cook than even Mom."

"For shame!"

The blue eyes danced.

Feeling guilty, Barbara added: "I didn't telephone the folks you'd be here this evening. They'd ask questions, and I thought possibly you'd been asked too many questions recently."

"I demand my garlic bread! I demand it!"

For a little while, oddly, Barbara had the feeling the clock had been turned backward a few years. How many times in the olden days she'd cooked for Andy and Andy had demanded garlic

61

bread! It was strange, that, because Andy was two years older and ought to have been the cook, not she. But even in those days, come to think of it, Andy had been much too busy preparing herself for fame to bother about learning to cook. Once, Barbara recalled, she'd asked Andy what would happen if she *didn't* have the career of her dreams. Andy had laughed. "But I must," she'd said, "because who'll cook for me if I can't pay her a decent salary?"

Andy ate all her salad and then cleaned up the remnants in the mixing bowl. Andy turned with gusto to the grilled chicken and shoestring potatoes and canned peas. "Try doing the peas with cubed ham," she suggested. "Mr. Hogan's cook does 'em that way, and they're delectable."

"Who's Mr. Hogan?"

"Bruce? Well, now, there's a tricky question. The New York newspapers often ask that question editorially. Who knows the answer? I'm sure that I don't. He came to the stage door one evening and asked Mr. Gustine to deliver a little gift to me in my dressing room and tell me he was waiting in the cold night air. The gift was an antique ruby brooch, a quite lovely thing. So I made myself presentable and had Mr. Hogan shown in."

"And returned the brooch, I hope."

Andy looked astonished. "Why on earth would I do that? It wasn't a gift with strings attached; it was a tribute to my performance."

"But, *Andy*!"

"Britches, please don't be dull. The theater isn't Sather, and Mr. Hogan isn't one of our callow Sather males. These things are done. There's a type of man, who, in fact, feeds his vanity by escorting the latest female rage to places where he'll be seen and envied. They're men who can afford the high cost."

Barbara concentrated on her chicken for a while, not wanting to debate a subject she knew little about.

"Technically," Andy said, "Bruce Hogan is a speculator. Apparently he's quite good at it."

"What does he think of all this?"

"I really don't know. He did start to speak about it the other evening, but I told him not to be glum. Bruce is tolerable because he always does what I tell him to do."

"How do you accomplish that?"

Andy chuckled. "Now you mustn't pry, Britches. Even a sister must be allowed a few secrets."

A thump sounded on the starboard deck, a thump Barbara had been waiting for. "I asked Hugh to come over for dessert," she said casually. "We were always a threesome, remember?"

Andy's face revealed nothing for a moment, and then the lovely brow wrinkled and she asked: "Was that a shrewd idea, do you think? The fewer who know I'm here, the less we'll be bothered."

"Oh, everyone in town should know

by now that you're here. I'll explain that later."

Hugh knocked, slid the door open and stepped into the salon. He made a grand sight this evening in steel-gray trousers and blue gaucho shirt, his black hair freshly trimmed and lustrous, his gray eyes lively with pleasure. "Do I say hello or hail or what?" he asked Andy. "I've never associated with a Broadway star, you know."

Andy laid her fork down and slipped from the stool and went to him lightly and gracefully and rose on tiptoe and kissed Hugh on the chin. "Now I'm home," Andy said with touching satisfaction. "That's good. Shall I quote you from a play by the great Goethe?"

She was before the fire, striking a pose, before anyone could say yes or no. Softly, with haunting sadness, she intoned:

"Oh, yes! A time will come! You children live only in the present and give no ear to our experience. Youth and happy love, all has an end; and there comes a time when one thanks God if one has any corner to creep into."

Andy turned with a ravishing smile. "But it must be a quiet corner to creep into, you understand, a corner of the Eastern Shore, with a good sister to do the cooking and a good friend to chat with while the chicken is being grilled."

Touched, Barbara told her to get back there on the stool and finish the chicken. She poured coffee for Hugh. She supposed this was as good a time as any to confess that she'd not had time to prepare a proper dessert. She made the confession somewhat embarrassedly, but Hugh dismissed the matter with a shrug. "We could all drive to the drugstore for a banana split," he said, "if anyone wants one. They'll be glad to see you there, Andy. Mr. Wells still tells the tourists that one summer Miss Andrea Lawrence worked as a waitress there."

"That was a summer," Andy said. "I must tell you there are times when men and boys can be a dreadful bother. When a girl's on the job, the men and boys ought to allow her to work at that job."

"Sometimes," Hugh said, "beauty tends to make a man giddy. I feel that way now about boats, especially about yawls of my own design and manufacture."

"Come to think of it," Andy said, "you must make me a yawl! Hugh, how exciting! Remember how we used to sit watching your father steam the planks just so for those elegant yachts he used to make? Now the children are adults, and another Robards yawl goes down to sea."

The telephone rang. Barbara answered, thinking it might be their mother. Instead, a rather musical bass voice asked: "Is this the baby sister, I wonder? This is Bruce Hogan, a friend of Miss Lawrence's. Did she get there all right?"

"Fine, Bruce. Andy's been telling me about you."

"Nice things, I hope."

"Nice things and interesting things. Care to wait a moment? I'll call Andy."

"Whoa, don't bother about that. I just wanted to know that she got there all right."

Barbara asked hopefully, "I don't know if she's all right, Bruce. She hasn't told me anything about the reason for all this, and of course I'm worried about the lawsuit."

"Never worry about Andy, Miss Holman. There's a girl who can look after herself."

"The trouble is," Barbara persisted, "that I know a different Andy. At high school, for example, Andy was much too adept at starting things she couldn't finish. Then Hugh or some other boy had to go to her rescue."

"I'll be the hero now."

"Wonderful! Why don't you come down soon, Bruce? If you've never been on the Eastern Shore, you have a treat in store for you."

"Maybe I'll do that, Miss Holman. Thanks for asking. I'll let you know; all right?"

"Fine."

Barbara returned to the salon and found it empty. Puzzled, she headed for the starboard deck. Andy's voice stopped her, however. Quite stridently, Andy said: "I'm so confused, Hugh, so dreadfully confused. You're supposed to feel happy when you've attained Broadway stardom, but I don't feel at all happy. Suddenly I had to get away. It was do that or go stark, staring mad. But I'm still not happy. I — "

The rest was lost in a queer outcry and then the sound of sobs. Hugh said, "Hush, darling. You're here now, so hush."

Barbara went back to the galley. Thoughtful, she took the dishes from the counter, then poured herself another cup of coffee.

6

THE following morning, at Andy's insistence, Barbara had the houseboat telephone disconnected temporarily. Barbara also telephoned the editor of the *Sather Record* and asked for enough of his time to make an appeal to his chivalry. Mr. Keyes invited her to come to his office during her lunch hour. When she got there he was blue-penciling copy in the manner of a man who wondered why he'd ever elected to write and publish a small-town weekly newspaper. "This yarn I'm working on," he said dourly, "has been on Peter Jay Nock's desk more often than it's been on mine. Mr. Nock would prefer that I print no copy about the Snively affair. Understandable, of course. But just as he has a duty to his clients, I have a duty to my readers."

Barbara sat down self-consciously. "I'm afraid I'm here to keep another story out of the paper, Mr. Keyes," she told him. "I suppose everyone in town knows that Andy is here, but Andy would be grateful if you didn't print the information."

His head snapped back. "When did she arrive? This is the first I've heard about it."

"Last evening, Mr. Keyes. Peter and I picked her up in Easton."

"How can I ignore a story like that? The national press services would pay big money for that story. If I did a story complete with pictures, I could sell it for bigger money to one of the picture magazines."

"It would complicate her life, you see."

Mr. Keyes took off his green eyeshade. A plump pale-faced man in his late thirties, he shook his balding head. "Can't be done," he said. "Listen to me a moment, please. When a woman becomes a glamour creature, a Broadway star, she loses her right to privacy. She's a public figure, fair game for any and all reporters or sob sisters or magazine writers. And that's fair, mind you, because you can't become a glamour creature, a Broadway star, a public figure, without the aid of the press. Anyone who accepts the rewards of free publicity has to accept the penalties of being a public figure."

"Andy was sure, sir, that no one in Sather would make things difficult for a Sather girl."

"Baloney. Your sister knows better than that or she'd not be a star. She's just trying baloney."

"But — "

"When may I interview her, Barbara? Certainly I won't write a sensational yarn, and certainly I'll not criticize her in any way. Still, I have to write that she's here, and I have to print any information I can get about her plans."

"She'd not receive you, sir."

He smiled rather boyishly. "I'm

positive she'd rather not receive me, Barbara. She has little option, however. If I telephone the regional office of one of the wire services, everyone in the country will know within a few hours that Miss Andrea Lawrence has holed up in her sister's houseboat in Sather, Maryland. By evening, reporters for press and radio and television will be in Sather. Cameras will be aimed at the houseboat. Reporters will probably try to climb aboard. The longer they're kept waiting for interviews, under those circumstances, the angrier they'll become. Some of the yarns will be downright unpleasant."

Barbara's lips tightened.

Mr. Keyes said sympathetically, "I'm afraid you're the kid sister in the middle again, Barbara. Look, I doubt you understand much of this, so let me tell you a few things. First of all, there's a strong likelihood that a top Broadway musical will fold in a few weeks because the star walked out. A lot of folks will be left unemployed; a lot of other folks won't make money selling tickets, renting hotel rooms, and such. And then — "

"Andy isn't well."

"Now, now, now."

"You won't just ignore the story?"

"I simply can't. News is news and must be printed. Do I interview Andy this afternoon, or do I telephone one of the wire services?"

"Mr. Keyes, that's practically blackmail!"

"I don't see that, Barbara. Consider the Snively affair. They're little people, very little people. This yarn about them will finish them here in Sather. It isn't pleasant to have to write such a yarn when you know what its effect will be. But it's my job. So if I don't suppress this yarn, how can I suppress the yarn involving Andy?"

Dismayed, Barbara sent Tad Ott to the houseboat with Mr. Keyes' ultimatum. When Tad returned, he was grinning and shaking his head. "Boy, Miss Holman," he marveled, "your sister can sure blow up."

"Well, she's going through a trying time. Will she see Mr. Keyes?"

"I guess she's seeing him right now, Miss Holman. Mr. Keyes drove up just as I was leaving."

"I see. Well, back to the stockroom, Tad. You and I are ordinary folks, remember, who have to earn our bread with hard work."

They spent much of the afternoon carrying things to and from the stockroom and setting up the spring and summer displays. For several hours there were few interruptions, but things changed after Tad had stepped shoeless into one of the show windows to arrange the bathing-suit and beach display. Several girls loped over to jeer at poor Tad, and then several teen-age fellows came along to make matters worse for him. All the noise attracted the attention of some adults, and presently the store was well filled with people who looked over the stock and made a few purchases and asked the customary questions about Andy's abrupt departure from the cast of *I Found A Daisy*. The nature of the questions changed abruptly, however, after one of the houseboat-cleaning girls came in and asked in a tizzy if Andrea Lawrence had loved sleeping in the spanking clean stateroom. Three women asked if poor Andy wanted to taste real Eastern Shore cooking again, and each of the ladies invited Andy and Barbara for dinner that very evening. Barbara managed to turn down the invitations tactfully, but there were other invitations and still more invitations and still more invitations.

Things grew worse after some of the women had gotten the opportunity to spread the news around town. Mrs. Leroy Nock, Peter's mother, telephoned from the great family estate on the outskirts of Sather. Barbara simply must scoop up that fascinating sister of hers that very moment and come to Shadow Lawn for dinner and talk that very evening. Peter could pick them up. Peter! Imagine a woman's own son keeping secret from her the fact that lovely Andrea Lawrence had returned to Sather!

"Andy's rather tired, Mrs. Nock," Barbara answered, beginning to tire of the excuse. "I'm sure that later on she'll love to visit Shadow Lawn. She needs rest right now, though."

"Barbara, I won't accept a refusal. I've been fascinated by the story ever since it was first made public. And don't forget I have a right to know the story behind the story. I was one of Andy's first fans and sponsors."

In fact, Barbara remembered, Mrs. Nock had perhaps done more than anyone else on earth to place Andy's feet on the road to stardom. Andy's first dancing lessons had been paid for by Mrs. Nock. Andy's first singing lessons had been paid for by Mrs. Nock. And in all probability, although Andy had never told her so, Andy's first trip to New York had been financed by Mrs. Nock.

"Not this evening," Barbara said firmly. "Some time soon, Mrs. Nock, but not this evening."

By the time she'd hung up, Barbara was worn out. She had Tad clear the store and close the door fifteen minutes early. She went up-river a couple of hundred feet to her parents' white-frame house on Elm Point, and when she'd achieved the cool, quiet porch she sank gratefully into one of the wicker armchairs and hollered to her mother that she had a daughter who could use a strong glass of iced tea. Her mother bustled out with a glass of lemonade, instead. A spare, graying, brown-eyed blonde woman of forty-nine, Edna Holman took a cushion to the stoop and sat on it, her back to Barbara. "I'm not sure I adore Andy just now," she said ruefully. "Such a daughter! We spent most of the afternoon discussing the horrible things I've done to your life."

"What?"

"It's Andy's opinion that we should

never have helped you open that store. You're a tank-town girl going nowhere, according to Andy. She claims we should have sent you to college so that you'd be qualified for an important business career in New York."

"Nonsense."

"Also, according to Andy, you're too fat, too complacent, too dowdy, and much too non-competitive for your own good."

"I'll go drown myself," Barbara volunteered. "How's that?"

Laughing, mother turned to daughter. "I made the error of disagreeing with everything Andy said. Andy told me not to be difficult, that she abhors difficult people."

"Were you there when Mr. Keyes arrived?"

"Yes. It was quite a performance, Britches. I understand now why Andy's such a success on the stage. She can dissemble beautifully, believe you me. She was so sweet, so modest, so girlishly troubled that Mr. Keyes was charmed.

I'm sure he didn't get much of a story from Andy."

"Lord, I hope you're wrong, Mom. Either he gets the full story or he relays his information to people who'll get the full story or bust."

"Has she told you the full story?"

"No. She was tired last evening, and I didn't think it was the time for questions."

"The story is Hugh Robards, dear."

Barbara sipped more lemonade, anxious to do something with her hands.

"I know Andy rather well, you see," Mrs. Holman explained. "I think that what she always planned was to marry Hugh as soon as she'd established herself on the stage."

"And here she is to achieve the second part of her dream?"

"Not consciously. I'm sure that Andy wouldn't consciously come here to scrap with her sister for Hugh. She's always loved you deeply, you know. Or did you know?"

"I don't think that would deter Andy if she wanted Hugh, Mom. Andy prides herself on her ability to go after whatever she wants without concern for herself or anyone else. By the way, Mrs. Nock has commanded an appearance this evening at Shadow Lawn. I couldn't outtalk her. Now what do I do?"

"You don't go. I suppose that somewhere behind the invitation was a hint that your business hopes could be furthered by Mrs. Leroy Nock if she spoke the right word?"

"It wasn't a hint, Mom. It was a flat statement."

"I don't see why you want to become part of the Nock retail chain. I went over your books last month, don't forget. You cleared almost eight thousand dollars. For a girl with only herself to support, and aboard a houseboat at that, you have a nice income."

"I'd like to buy the property next to the store, Mom, and broaden my line, my trade. To do that, I need to get out of the homesy-womesy setup I now have. The Nock line's a darned good line. They offer quality merchandise, a lot of support advertising, and attractive credit."

"You see, dear, I don't want you to become too involved in a business operation just before you marry Hugh. The marriage should have your full attention, I think."

"It would be part of our total operation, Mom. Things are slow at the boat yard during the winter, as you know. On the other hand, the store does a nice year-round business. So the two businesses would complement one another and give us greater security."

"The boat yard earns a nice income, however."

As if her mother hadn't spoken, Barbara went on musingly, "And then, I suppose, I do have ambition in my way just as Andy has in hers. I love having my own business. It's a challenge, really, to anticipate the needs of people and to meet those needs completely and profitably."

"Then, of course, you grab Andy and make that command appearance at Shadow Lawn."

Barbara's large brown eyes swung to her mother's face. "I've been wondering, though, if a show of independence isn't in order, Mom. After all, I don't really *need* the Nock line."

Vincent Holman came home from the day's work, swinging his lunch box and whistling. "Lots of excitement down around the *River Lark*," he reported. "Constable Allard has a deputy on duty."

"Oh, no Sather person will bother Andy, Pop."

"Some of those reporters aren't Sather people, though."

Sighing, Barbara got up to help Andy defend her right to privacy. She wished, though, that Andy hadn't come to Sather for the reason her mother had guessed. After all, she thought unhappily, Andy had had her chance. What right had Andy to wreck so many lives and even careers for a chance to try again?

7

THE newspaper stories originating in Sather, Maryland, interested director Abner Wallace of Grapnis Television Features, Incorporated. He had his secretary clip each day's story from the *Los Angeles Times* and file it in a special folder in the lower left-hand drawer of his desk. As the folder thickened, Abner developed the notion that the beautiful and talented Andrea Lawrence was up for grabs, professionally speaking, if a fellow could just think up a gimmick. Surely, he thought, he was just the rat to think up the gimmick. God hadn't just picked him up by the scruff of the neck and set him down in this plushy office off Wilshire Boulevard. No, sir! Abner Wallace sat where he sat because all his life he'd been rat enough to think up a gimmick when a gimmick would do him some good.

Moira stepped in, slinkily feline this day in a lightweight beige dress wrought of knit wool. "Are you thinking?" Moria asked. "If you're thinking, sir, I apologize for interrupting."

"You're lovely. Have I told you so?"

"Yes, sir. That's why you hired me, sir, recall? You said it was a poor office that couldn't afford the luxury of one beautiful but stupid secretary."

"I never called you stupid. That would be ungallant. I'm many undesirable things, but never ungallant."

"The reason I came in without knocking, sir, is that Mr. Grapnis has elected to spare you ten seconds of his time."

Abner felt a chill stab to his toes. Mechanically, he reached into a desk drawer for a Tums. When he could speak unquaveringly, he asked: "Did he say why he wants to see me?"

"I think he's unhappy with the ratings of your two shows, sir."

Abner took another Tums. "I specifically remember predicting failure, Moria, if casting didn't give me the feminine leads I asked for. I specifically recall saying that the feminine leads in both shows had to be women with a very delicate touch."

"Sir, Mr. Grapnis' third secretary said that you're not to blame casting for the failures."

"Of course not! Who's the head of casting? His nephew! Who's agent for those two dogs they stuck me with? His niece!"

"You'll be late, sir, if you don't hurry."

Abner put on his two-hundred-dollar jacket and straightened the wings of his sixty-dollar bow tie. He went upstairs to the executive suite and announced himself to the receptionist. To his horror, he was taken through office after office at once until he was face to face with the great man himself in a great, quiet, shadowed office with beautifully stained glass windows imported from Belgium. Mr. Grapnis said generously, "Whoever you are, young man, sit down. I don't like to bend my neck, to tell the truth."

"It's generous of you to receive me, Mr. Grapnis."

"So!"

"And it's especially generous of you, sir, to give me the benefit of your broad knowledge. Frankly, I need help both with *Turtle Bay* and *Scream, Eagle!* There's a big idea, a valid idea, in both stories, I believe. We've just not realized on the potential."

"Oh, you're Wallace. I knew I'd seen you before. Wallace, how come you're directing two dogs and still working for Grapnis? Are you a conniver? Is that what you are? Have you sweet-talked my niece into fighting to keep you on the payroll?"

"No, sir."

"Wallace, I'm unhappy. I'm sincerely unhappy. I give you top writers, top actresses and actors, and even prime time. So what happens? You're not in the first thirty with either show!"

"Well, sir, as I've said, sir — "

"No, Wallace. I'll do the saying, all right? I mean, I have the right. Whoever's driving the custom-made Jaguar, Wallace, is the fellow who has the right to do the saying. That's life. Don't blame me. Blame life."

"Yes, sir."

Mr. Grapnis pressed a button. His first secretary came in. She had in her hands a large file folder lettered: *Abner Wallace*. Mr. Grapnis told her to resumé Wallaces' accomplishments for him, and the secretary did. It gave Abner pleasure to listen. He'd made his mark in television, all right. Two shows he'd directed had won awards. Eight out of ten shows he'd directed had finished among the top fifteen in all the ratings reports issued by the top rating agencies. He'd never directed a sustainer.

"I owe it all to the talent and facilities you provide," he said humbly to Mr. Grapnis when the woman had finished reading. "This is quite an organization, sir, if I may say so."

"What's wrong, Wallace? Have you gone stale?"

"No, sir. Basically, we have difficult story lines in both shows. Unless you have just the correct woman in each of the leading parts — "

"Such as?"

"Andrea Lawrence, for one, sir. *Turtle Bay* needs her sparkle, her voice."

"Who's Andrea Lawrence?"

"The actress who's walked out of *I Found A Daisy*, sir."

"A contract breaker? You want me to hire a contract breaker? Wallace, I don't think I like you a whole lot."

"It isn't established, sir, that she's broken a contract. She's arguing she was discharged by Mark Banes because he was dissatisfied with her performance."

"You want me to hire a poor performer? Wallace, I don't think I like you even a little bit."

"Mark Banes, sir, has had trouble

with other stars both on Broadway and here in Hollywood. This organization once discharged Mark Banes because he almost ruined a spectacular before it could be taped."

"So!"

The gimmick came to Mr. Abner Wallace, a gimmick so beautiful he almost cried out in admiration. He said softly, casually, "Miss Lawrence may or may not be able to prove her argument in court, sir, but it really isn't relevant. She's presently at liberty, and she's much in the news because of the walkout *and* her great performance in *I Found A Daisy*. I should think she'd be interested in taping thirteen shows or so for us over the summer. Regardless of the outcome of her argument with Banes, we'd have her on tap — an easy item to market."

"So!"

"The idea will occur to someone else, sir," Abner said with increasing confidence. "I hope we can get her for *Turtle Bay*."

The black eyes of Patrick Grapnis communed for a while with the stained glass window depicting St. George in mortal combat with a dragon's head. "You aren't dumb," he said at length. "Not that I'd pay you a penny more, but you have a pretty good record, Wallace. If you think *Turtle Bay* can go another year, I'll string along with you. This contract breaker, though — I get nervous when I even think of doing business with a contract breaker."

"Sir, I wonder if maybe I should go East and investigate the entire situation. Frankly, I think that Miss Lawrence must have a pretty good argument. What did she amount to before she hit it big in *I Found A Daisy*? She had two walk-ons; then she was fifth banana in an off-Broadway musical that laid an egg. People don't throw away a smash hit like *I Found A Daisy* unless they have an argument going for them."

Mr. Grapnis shrugged. "I always give my directors enough rope to hang themselves. Wallace. If you want to go East, make the arrangements. One thing's for sure, though. *Scream, Eagle!* is dead. After six years of it, I'm too tired of it to pump new blood into its veins."

Abner Wallace winced, as would any man who'd just lost half his income.

Patrick Grapnis was amused. "Son," he said, "let me tell you why it's a privilege for little punks like you to work for me. I have a mind that never forgets. I never forget a flop or a failure or an in-between. If a punk has a good record, I don't chop off his fingers so he can't eat. I have a couple of ideas jelling at the back of my brain. I like one of them a whole lot, because the original idea was thought up by my niece. She's a talented girl, Leota, don't you think?"

"I sincerely admire her talent, sir. I'm sure everyone knows that."

"One thing that convinces me of that, Wallace, is that you didn't try to blame your stars for these failures. After all, my niece is agent for those stars, and blaming them would have been like blaming her. Okay. I'm glad we've had this constructive chat. We'll keep *Turtle Bay*, and we'll work the contract breaker into the new show if you're able to prove to me she's worthy of working for Grapnis. We'll dump *Scream, Eagle!* I'll get my niece to develop her idea for a new show a bit more fully, and then I'll put you to work on that. Meanwhile, you keep your salary and office."

"Thank you, sir."

"I'm like that," Patrick Grapnis marveled. "How can a great man be so kind?"

He waved a dismissal, and Abner left quickly. He went directly to the travel office and had them arrange for transportation to New York. Late that same evening he was aboard a New York plane, and at ten o'clock the following morning he walked into the reception room of Simon Levine's office suite on Madison Avenue and told the girl to tell Simon he was a Grapnis director looking for a star. He was shown into a small, austerely furnished office and subjected to a long, brown-eyed stare and then a noncommittal smile. "*Turtle Bay*; *Scream, Eagle!*" Levine said. "How come you're still working for Grapnis, Wallace? The book I have on Grapnis says that he dumps the directors of flops."

"Don't forget, Levine, that they've both been on television for years."

"Sure. What are you planning — a new show?"

"Could be. Also, we've decided to alter the story line of *Turtle Bay*. We want a fresh face, a fresh talent."

"That's understandable. I don't like to knock anybody, but the girl you've got in the lead this year — well, television isn't her field."

Abner Wallace sat down and lighted a cigarette. "I was thinking about Andrea Lawrence, Levine."

The brown eyes blinked.

"She's young, beautiful, talented," Abner said. "We could shift production to New York, if need be, and tape a block of shows without interfering in any way with her other commitments."

Simon Levine visibly wrestled with his conscience. Abner liked the man for that. Show business was a tough business. Any time you met an agent who had a conscience, you met a rare person.

"I know about her," Abner said shortly. "I have it figured that she has a pretty good argument in favor of doing what she did. Nobody gets off the top rung of the ladder just for kicks."

"Well, Andy's an odd girl. Lots of personality and beauty and talent. She has a special way of looking at things, though."

"Banes has had trouble before. Let me guess what happened — and you tell me if I'm right. At rehearsals, he sweated her. He hammered away until he got the performance exactly as he wanted it. But the performance, as he wanted it, was a bit stiff, didn't play, as we say. So, being a talented person, Miss Lawrence made the adjustments any good actress makes to keep the performance easy and natural. Banes blew his stack. His way, or else. Now, then, am I right?"

The agent asked, puzzled: "Were you there?"

"Banes used to be in Hollywood, you know. I saw him work. He's the Napoleon type. Well, a sensitive star can't stand him for long, and I'd guess that Miss Lawrence is sensitive."

"Still," Levine said, "there's that contract."

"Is television forbidden?"

"No."

"So there you are, Levine."

"So how do you know she won't do to *Turtle Bay* what she's done to *I Found A Daisy*?"

Abner Wallace smiled radiantly. "I'm just rat enough, Levine," he bragged, "to come up with a gimmick whenever I need one. Do you know what my gimmick is here? It's very simple, and beautiful in its simplicity. The one thing your Andrea Lawrence won't dare to do is have trouble with me. Right now, because everybody in the business knows about Banes, she's getting the benefit of some doubt. But if she has more trouble on top of that Banes trouble, she can kiss her career bye-bye. So I know she won't do to *Turtle Bay* what she's done to *I Found A Daisy*. She'd have to be crazy to do that, and I don't think she's crazy."

"What kind of money are we discussing, by the way?"

"Two thousand a show, or twenty-six thousand for the block of thirteen."

"Mr. Wallace, good morning."

Abner smiled and waited, knowing that Levine had no bargaining position at the moment. The girl *had* to do something, and soon, to establish that her talent was for real and that she was more stable than she seemed to be at present. Lord, Abner thought, what a gimmick he'd hatched this time!

"If you drive a hard bargain now," Levine pointed out, "you can't complain if we drive a harder one when you want to renew. It's up to you, Wallace."

Abner rose, grinning. "I may be more generous," he said, "after I've met Miss Lawrence. Set it up, will you?"

8

ON May twelfth Barbara was unpleasantly surprised by a brisk letter from Simon Levine ordering her to find accommodations for himself and an Abner Wallace at 'some decent place' without letting Andy know they were coming down to Sather. Tad noticed her expression and asked: "Bad news, Miss Holman? Hey, why don't I be your secretary? I could sort the good from the bad and feed you the bad when it won't wreck your day."

Barbara suggested that perhaps he ought to hurry the morning cleaning. At least ten persons were waiting outside for the store to open, and three looked quite prosperous. Tad said he'd already done the morning cleaning and challenged Barbara to find one speck of dust he'd overlooked.

Meeting his China blue eyes, Barbara decided not to accept the challenge. In Master Ott, she was beginning to realize, she'd found a prize. Even if by some miracle Charles Snively were to be turned loose by the authorities, she'd have to keep Tad in her employ. The boy had a future in the retail business. He was quick, he was industrious, and he was always thinking.

"My apologies," she said, smiling. "You mustn't spoil me, you know. I don't hire you to wear yourself out."

Tad glanced at the wall clock beyond her desk. "It's better cleaning up just before I go to school," he said. "That way, things look nice when you open up. If I clean up at the end of the day, things don't look so good."

"How are your grades, incidentally? Charles had trouble maintaining his grades."

"I'll get practically a full point, I guess. I figure I'll end my junior year with a 2.8 average."

Barbara's brown brows arched.

"Really? That's quite good."

"We've got a girl at school, Miss Holman, who'll end up this year with a full four points. Talk about the scholarships she'll win!"

"Do you plan to go to college?"

"Well, I'm not sure. I like this kind of business, and you don't have to go to college to open a store. My folks claim, though, that I'll have more of a choice of a career if I do go to college."

"That's true."

"But you take your sister, Miss Holman. I read in one of the papers that she's earning a lot more than a hundred thousand a year. All she did was go to high school."

"Oh, but that's not true! Andy's had singing and dancing lessons for many years. When she went to New York, she attended an acting school. Then she went into a repertory company in Connecticut for fuller training. In her field she's had more than the equivalent of undergraduate college work."

"Say, I'd better tell some of the girls that! I know five girls who plan right now to be stars instead of going to college."

Barbara laughed. "Sure," she said, "why study when you can earn a million a year by dreaming?" She turned to the telephone and made reservations for that weekend for Mr. Levine and Mr. Wallace at the Sather Inn. Tad went out the back door and hopped aboard his bike and pedaled off to school. She watched him speed along the river road to its junction with Rodway Street. She loved the free and easy way he rode that bike; she rather envied him his youth and his freedom from real worry and his headful of boyish dreams. It was strange, she thought, how the life you ultimately led bore little resemblance to the life you dreamed about as a teen-ager. She herself had once dreamed of being a nurse. Andy, of course, had attained some of her dream — yet even there the thing attained hadn't quite come up to the dream. Surely Andy had never dreamed that in stardom, for instance, she'd find unhappiness!

Someone knocked on the door. Barbara checked the clock, flushed, and opened up hurriedly. The third person to step inside was Carol Robards, a chunky nineteen whose gray eyes would never be as quiet as her brother's. While the shoppers spread through the store, Carol set her handbag on the counter near the cash register and asked with soft tenseness: "Barbara, what's happening? Every time I see Hugh, he's either just going to visit Andy or coming away from a visit with her."

"Well, she's lonely, you know. It can't be much fun for her to be holed up on the *River Lark*."

"Is there a law that says she has to remain aboard? Is there a law that says Hugh has to neglect his business to prevent her from boring herself to death?"

"I didn't know he was neglecting his business."

"Well, he is! I went to the boatyard the other afternoon, and he wasn't there. I talked with Mr. Jenks. Mr. Jenks was upset because they have four boats that need Hugh's personal attention, and he can't get Hugh to work."

"Really?"

"All of 'em have engine trouble," Carol explained. "You know Hugh. If Dad did anything at all for Hugh, he made Hugh the top marine engine mechanic in Maryland."

"Crack the whip!"

Carol asked dolefully: "How do I do that when I seldom catch up with him?"

A young fellow came to the counter with a scuba diving outfit. Barbara didn't recognize him, so she went to her office for maps of the Sather River, the Tred Avon River, the Choptank River, and the various creeks of the region. The fellow was quite pleased. "I've been wondering where I'd get these maps," he said. "Will a check be all right? I have lots of identification."

Barbara handed him a pen. A few moments later she rang up her first sale of the day — a fat one amounting to forty-four dollars and sixty-nine cents.

After the customer had left, Carol asked: "Is it a good idea to accept checks from strangers? We've had to return several checks recently."

"I'm insured against loss. And this is an odd business, Carol. If you don't accept checks for the larger purchases, you just don't make the larger sales. I have few losses, come to think of it."

"Just Hugh, eh?"

"Hugh?"

The gray eyes of young Carol Robards were very stormy now. "It should be pretty clear," she snapped, "what's happening with Hugh and Andy. You surprise me! You always claim to be such a realist, but when a thing like this happens you don't even see it."

"Whoa, Carol. Naturally they're seeing

a great deal of one another. They were good friends, don't forget. That doesn't mean, though, that I'm losing Hugh to Andy."

"When did you have your last date with him?"

Barbara gave it thought. "The week before Andy came, I believe. Why?"

"You're supposed to be married next month, but you've not had a real date with Hugh in more than a month. I should think that would make you wonder. I know that I'd wonder if Randy treated me that way."

"Well, this is Hugh's busy time, you know."

"Then why," asked Carol sharply, "is he goofing off at the boat yard?"

It was a good question, of course, a question as entirely logical as Carol was about everything. The girl, Barbara thought, should have become a teacher rather than a bank teller. Certainly there were many in Sather who needed to be taught to reason logically from a premise. Still, she reflected, it was foolish to apply the reasoning processes of logic in a purely emotional situation. In a sense, to do that was like trying to measure a square mile with an ohm. The ohm simply couldn't be used that way, period.

Carol smiled faintly, somewhat apologetically. "I know you're older and wiser than I, Barbara," she said. "I do want you as a sister-in-law, though. I worry."

"It's nice of you to be concerned, Carol. I'd not worry, though. I imagine that Andy seems very glamorous to Hugh just now. I imagine, too, that she's awakened many memories. It's fun to turn the clock backward a few years, I suppose. I never have, but Hugh does so frequently. Still, they're not high school girl and boy any more, are they?"

Carol glanced at her wristwatch. She'd already made her mark at the Sather Bank because she was both able and dependable. Carol could no more report late for work than she could behave her age at a beach party. She smoothed her black hair and stole a quick glance at her reflection in the wall mirror. "I hope you know what you're doing," she said. A moment later she was headed purposefully across the road, in the crosswalk, of course, en route to the brick bank building.

The early rush of business petered out. To avoid thinking about the things Carol had reported, Barbara went along the four aisles of her broad, deep store to check the counters and various racks. It interested her to see that Tad had quickly caught on to her work methods. Merchandise which had been sold the previous day had been replaced from stock. In the stockroom itself, Tad had carefully filled in the replacement list and had also subtracted the merchandise drawn from stock from the stockroom inventory. He'd also left a note saying, "Swim fins are in with the high school bunch — better order some more." Carol checked the proper shelf and found she had only ten sets of swim fins left. As she checked other shelves, she made the interesting discovery that much of her stock was low despite the fact she'd received a big order just a few days before Charles had been arrested. The discovery sent her hustling to her office to look over the past month's sales. The figures startled her, as did the size of her business account at the bank. Glory be, she thought, she'd clear more than twelve thousand this year if business held up like that a couple of months more!

Now, all her thoughts concentrated upon business, she telephoned Peter Jay Nock at his office. Peter came on after a short wait to declare: "My favorite brunette! I hope you're not checking on the Snively case, because there's nothing to report."

"So you reported yesterday," she reminded him. "I'm calling about another matter. Peter, I don't suppose you could tell me what your father's decided on about that lease thing I discussed with you two?"

"The old boy hasn't mentioned it to me. I think my mother's offended because Andy and you never did show up one evening."

"I warned her that Andy was tired."

"My mother wants what she wants when she wants it. A splendid woman, you understand — but Dad's indulged her."

"Peter, this is a business matter, after all. And I have to know what the decision will be, because I'm about to reorder. If I telephone my regular distributor, I'll have my stock replaced within a week. Once it's been replaced, I'll not be able to make a change until it's been disposed of."

"What are you doing — running a sale?"

"Peter, I've already made the best sales talk I can think of.

"Nope. Business is just a lot better this year than last year."

"Can you wait until Sunday?"

"If your father isn't sold now, he won't be sold on Sunday."

Peter hemmed and hawed a while and then told her he'd call back within the half-hour. While she was waiting for the call, Barbara opened the office window to the river breeze and leaned out to check the backyard garden. The petunias and snapdragons were coming along fine, she saw, but the roses still looked as roses ought not to look in any town possessed of an active and rather zealous garden club. She decided that if Mr. Nock's answer were yes, she'd be able to afford a part-time gardener — perhaps one of the high school kids who'd be looking for a summer job. Another thing she'd do, she thought, was give serious consideration to cutting another entrance into the store. The river road was traveled heavily in the summer, so that it might be profitable for her to take down the back fences, stretch a brick path to the road, and have a pretty entrance constructed by her father. Then —

Peter's call drew her to the desk in a hurry. "You owe me a dinner and a kiss," Peter announced. "I'll settle for a kiss."

"Peter!"

"Actually," Peter said, "Dad's happy to have an outlet in our town. You're to draw up a list of the stock you need forthwith and telephone the order collect to our Baltimore warehouse. In a couple of days you'll get the standard contract we have with retail stores throughout the country. Dad will see to ordering the sign right away. My, you go-getter, you!"

On an impulse Barbara asked: "Will you settle for a dinner, Peter? Not aboard the *River Lark*, you understand. Darn it, I *am* grateful."

"To please you," Peter said, "I'd even marry you. Think of that!"

"The trouble is, you see — "

But Peter, interrupting, got the last word. "I see the trouble, all right,"

Peter said. "What bothers me is that you don't see it. See you Saturday at six."

He hung up before Barbara could sputter.

9

LIKE a pretty, well-fed, contented cat, Andy sat up languorously on the chaise longue on the bow deck of the *River Lark*. Barbara waved as she went to the houseboat along the catwalk, and Andy called: "My, what a lovely sight! Darling, you're positively blooming!"

Off in a shaded corner of the deck sat Hugh Robards in swim trunks, his torso faintly pink and shining with moisture. Hugh said in his deliberate way, "I've brought lamb chops and a nice wine. The wine's chilling in the creek."

Barbara went to him for the customary kiss. Hugh did kiss her cheek after a fashion, but with a reluctance that was almost insulting. Barbara clung to her temper, but of course she didn't mislead Andy with her careful smile.

"Pet," Andy reproved Hugh, "you used at least to rise in the old days when a girl offered you her face. I abhor boors, I really do."

Barbara continued on to her stateroom. With the door closed and the curtains drawn, she relieved her feelings by flinging her handbag on her double bed. She started to change, but she thought better of that idea. She freshened up in the bathroom, then got her handbag again and went back to the bow deck. "You cook the chow," she told Andy. "I have business in town, so I'll eat at the Inn."

Hugh had apparently been scolded during her absence. He said resentfully, "That's just fine. A fellow brings the makings of a good dinner and ends up in the doghouse. Listen, Barbara, I'm tired. I had a tough job at the boat yard today. I came over for a swim and a nice dinner and — "

"Oh, did Carol catch up with you? She told me yesterday that you've been goofing off."

The gray eyes narrowed.

Barbara ambled back to the shore by way of the catwalk. She followed Jory Street to Lawrence Street and took Lawrence Street to the center of Sather. She was luckier than she'd hoped to be. As she passed Betty's Beauty Salon, little Betty popped out to ask what she was doing on the town. Barbara said she was doing nothing. Betty took her arm promptly. "Meet another bum," she said cheerfully. "I'll do nothing with you."

They walked on to Municipal Pier. The ferryboat was just coming in from Princess Anne, so there was a collection of townspeople and tourists on hand to see the sight. The ferry-boat, fat and spotlessly white, looked lovely against the water and sky. The steady plunk-plunk-plunk of its engine was music to the ears of a girl who'd heard the sound practically all her life. It had been on the deck of that same ferryboat, Barbara recalled, that she'd first realized she was in love with Hugh

Robards. That had been a moment to remember always.

"How's Andy?" Betty asked. "Some of my customers are all excited about her. The tourists, mainly. They can't understand why we local yokels don't make more of a fuss about her."

"Andy eats, sleeps, swims a little, watches television, and thinks long thoughts." Barbara looked at the redhead. "Much the same Andy you used to know, except that she has more self-confidence."

"I never noticed in the old days that she lacked self-confidence."

"Well, it's now manifested by a certain regality and a complete unconcern about her future. I don't mind saying I'm disturbed, Betty. The business world couldn't function a year if written and signed agreements weren't honored. Andy laughs at my old-fashioned notions, though."

"Maybe she shouldn't laugh. The reason I chased after you just now is that this morning I had a customer named Jane Creach. She's young and beautiful and smooth. It took me a whole minute to guess she'd come into the shop to pump me for information about Andy. It took me another whole minute to realize she's the same Jane Creach who writes a Broadway column that appears in one of the Easton papers, among others."

Barbara winced. "What sort of questions did she ask?"

"Oh, she asked what Andy was like as a child, as a teenager. She asked if any of us had ever guessed Andy would become a star. She wanted to know about men, of course. She got something there. Just as I was saying I knew of no romantic interest, Mrs. Wrightson said real loud: 'Oh, but you're wrong, dear — what about Hugh?' And I couldn't just laugh it off, either, because Mrs. Wrightson then went on to crack about Hugh spending so much time with Andy these days. I think Miss Creach felt she'd gotten her money's worth for the shampoo and set

I charged her for."

The boat bumped the pier very gently, and Mr. Wade flipped a line around a bitt and snubbed the boat short. He noticed Barbara and Betty watching him, and he grinned and waved, as if to show he bore them no hard feelings for the trouble they'd given him when they'd been tykes and he'd been constable of Sather. He ran the gangplank to the pier. Three cars rolled off the boat, and then a dozen or so foot passengers disembarked. Barbara, feeling quite hungry now, turned from the pier and looked thoughtfully up the street at the old Sather Inn. "Do you have a two-dollar appetite or a five-dollar appetite?" she asked Betty. "I'm celebrating an event, but I've only nine dollars with me."

"Suppose I buy my own dinner?"

"Suppose I pull that lovely red hair?"

"I have a three-dollar appetite," Betty said, grinning. "If you pay the tip, I'll buy the wine."

As it turned out, however, their

dinners were bought for them by none other than Jane Creach. The woman, diminutive and lovely and blonde, recognized her beautician in the lobby of the old Sather Inn. Betty introduced Barbara, and Miss Creach had heard of Miss Barbara Holman, of course. She insisted they dine with her in the Marine Room overlooking the Sather River. She ordered a filet mignon and grinningly told them she had an expense account and that they'd be crazy if they didn't order the same thing. They did with a promptitude that made her laugh warmly. "I adore you small-town girls," Miss Creach confided. "You're so healthily and attractively direct!"

She had news for Barbara, and she passed it along as they began on their crabmeat salad. "Things are coming to some sort of climax around here, Miss Holman," she started out. "This afternoon I spotted Simon Levine and Abner Wallace in the bar. An hour ago, I spotted the cause of the walkout, if your sister's to be believed. Mark Banes. Know him?"

"I've heard of him," Barbara said dryly. "I don't really know any of the people involved with Andy's career, however. I've met Mr. Levine twice, and he's been very nice to me, but I don't really know even him."

"Not interested in the theater, Miss Holman?"

"I'm afraid not, Miss Creach. I've always loved being a Sather girl. It's never occurred to me to live or work anywhere else."

"Lovely town."

"Have you met any of the Sathers? Old Mr. Sather established this town many years ago. He loved the setting, he didn't want it spoiled by heavy industry and the like, and he had the means to develop the town as he wanted to see it develop."

"You mean he just began it from nothing?"

Betty laughed. "Glory, no, Miss Creach. There was always a town of a kind here ever since Colonial days. But we were just a farming and fishing community, and the town certainly didn't amount to much. Mr. Sather put money into real estate and sold it off for nice homes, and then he put up this inn and some other places, and here we are. Naturally, the new town was called Sather."

"Andrea Lawrence disliked it, though." The words came out as a statement; not a question. "I wonder why?"

Barbara was puzzled. "I never knew Andy disliked Sather. She left, sure, but only because you can't have a career in the theater on the Eastern Shore."

Miss Creach said smoothly, "She once told me she hated this place, that she couldn't marry the fellow she wanted to marry because he was determined to remain in Sather. Naturally, I assumed she was telling the truth."

Barbara managed to say just as smoothly, "I never doubt my sister's veracity, Miss Creach. I was surprised, that's all."

Simon Levine came into the Marine Room with a tall, towheaded fellow who had wash gray eyes. Simon spotted them as he looked around for a table. He bustled over, his short, barrel-chested body seeming to exude animal energy. "Barbara," he said warmly, "it's been too long a time. A man's crazy not to come to Sather at least twice a year, and I kid you not."

Barbara introduced Betty, and Simon introduced Mr. Abner Wallace. Miss Creach insisted the men join them in a gustatorial assault against her expense account. It was instructive to Barbara to see Miss Creach at work. Hardly had the men ordered Martinis before Miss Creach was asking: "Are you the Abner Wallace of Grapnis Television, Mr. Wallace? I seem to recall your handsome face. I never forget a handsome face."

"I'm just rat enough to be a Grapnis

director, Miss Creach. But don't quote a man."

"Looking for talent down here, Mr. Wallace?"

Simon asked, "How much does a girl want just because she buys a fellow a drink?"

"What I want, Simon, of course, is a complete story on Andrea Lawrence. It's definite that *I Found A Daisy* will close, at least temporarily, unless she returns to the cast. Why? The thing fascinates me, and it fascinates the syndicate I work for. Here's a young and beautiful and quite talented young lady throwing her first major role away as if it were dirt. She's not rich — not yet. She's not established — not yet. She's the client of one of the shrewdest agents in the business. Knowing you, I know you've argued with her. Still, here she is, holed up on a houseboat in a tank-town creek as if she were fleeing from the law. Why? A very, very interesting question."

The men elected to have another

Martini each. Meanwhile, Betty and Barbara plodded on through their steak and baked potato and asparagus with Hollandaise sauce. Twice Betty made motions as if to leave, but each time Barbara shook her head sternly. Betty, of course, gleefully remained in the company of these famous and important people.

Simon turned to Barbara. "I met a lawyer today," he said, "who tells me you'll give him a reference. Ever hear of a guy named Peter Jay Nock?"

"Yes. Perhaps before I tell you he's very good, I should tell you that he wants to marry me."

Betty made a strangling sound.

"His father," Barbara went on cheerfully, "is Mr. Leroy Nock, founder and president of the Nock Retail Chain System. If you go to the foot of Frederick Street, you'll see two pink marble lions guarding a poplar-lined road into a lovely estate. The estate's called Shadow Lawn, and it's the lair of the Nocks — Peter included."

Simon asked practically, "Why's he a tank-town lawyer instead of lawyer for the company? Not very sharp?"

"He has to be sharp, Simon, since he does want to marry me."

Miss Creach chuckled and patted Barbara's hand. "Nicely put," she congratulated the girl. "Miss Holman, I begin to like you and even admire you. You have, shall we say, a most refreshing simplicity and honesty."

Abner Wallace said matter-of-factly, "One lawyer's as good as another in a deal like this, Levine. It's a standard contract, after all."

Barbara swung her eyes to Mr. Wallace. "You want Andy for television, sir?"

"I think so. If her terms are reasonable, that is."

"But how do we get to see her?" Simon asked. "I went to the houseboat. Your local slapstick cops have a guard on the catwalk who won't even take her a message."

Barbara saw, or thought she saw, a way out of the problem Andy was creating for her. She told the men to eat their dinners and then come aboard the houseboat with her. Miss Creach asked hopefully, "May I come, too?" Simon told her to be a big girl, but Barbara said flatly that no one could come with her if Miss Creach and Betty couldn't. In the end, they all rode to the creek in one of the Sather Inn limousines. Constable Allard's deputy called a cheery greeting to Barbara and Betty and stepped aside so they could enter the catwalk. Barbara yoo-hooed to give Andy and Hugh fair warning, but she might as well have saved her breath. The boat was empty, and Andy had left a tart note on the stove in the galley. The note read: "I abhor sulky people who leave others to starve. We may or may not be back."

Simon looked at the note Barbara thrust wordlessly into his hand. "It figures," Simon said. "She abhors a lot of people these days."

He took Mr. Wallace and Miss Creach back to town with him, and

Barbara and Betty went to chairs on the starboard deck. After a while, Betty said, "A lot of folks are talking about Hugh and Andy, Barbara. It's pretty plain to them that he's as loopy as he ever was about her."

"What do I do — shoot him?"

"Ah, now — "

Barbara Holman interrupted savagely, "I don't quit. I never quit. If Andy thinks I'm a quitter, she'll be sorry."

And yet, Barbara thought, how could you hate a lovely sister who'd always been kind and generous?

10

THE Saturday dinner with Peter Jay Nock was infinitely more pleasant than Barbara had expected it to be. Peter came to the catwalk in his Cadillac convertible a few minutes before six o'clock. No peremptory beeps from his horn! Rather, he came sedately aboard the houseboat and rang the gong once outside the main salon door. It was Andy who let him in, a thoughtful and strangely subdued young blonde woman who seemed particularly anxious to impress everyone with her good behavior. It was Andy who served the punch Barbara had prepared, and it was Andy who passed the snacks. "If I only knew how to cook," Andy said, "I'd do a meal for you two, really I would. Or if you'd just allow me to send for Mrs. Rennick, Barbara — "

"No, thanks. Speaking of food, there are any number of good restaurants in town, Andy. You needn't be afraid anyone will pester you. The folks of Sather do look after their own, you know."

"Well, I may dash pell-mell to the nearest place. I'm sorry we can't all dine together, though. I'd gladly buy."

Barbara waited gloomily for Peter to fall into Andy's trap. She was beginning to realize just how adept Andy was in the art of setting such traps. But Peter just said politely but definitely: "Two's company; three's a bore."

The dinner, it turned out, wouldn't cost Barbara a penny. Peter drove her straight to Shadow Lawn and refused to take no for an answer. Mr. and Mrs. Nock were lighting the Japanese lanterns on what they were pleased to call Marble Terrace, and Mr. Nock turned his part of the chore over to his son. He gripped Barbara's hand warmly. "I've never had a lovelier business colleague," he assured her.

"I hope you make a million dollars."

After all the lanterns had been lighted, Mrs. Nock turned on the fountains of the ornamental pool just beyond the marble flagstones. "Special effects for a special occasion," she said. "I do wish Andy could have come with you, however. I'm perishing to know the story behind the story."

"Well," Peter fibbed, "Andy had a headache, see, and her mood was foul."

"Poor child, the strain's been too much for her."

"You could say that," Peter conceded. "On the other hand, you could say other things."

He went off into the house with his mother, and Mr. Nock, sitting down, said with some apology, "I thought we might have a chat, you and I, before dinner. I think that what Peter wants me to do is warn you against allowing your sister to use you. Care to hear more, or shall I keep quiet? We have your welfare at heart, please remember."

Barbara nodded, knowing that was true. The fact was, the Nocks seemed to be interested in the welfare of just about every person in town. If they didn't have the longest charity list in Sather, it wasn't for lack of interest in helping people!

"Barbara," he said softly, "I received a curious letter from your sister yesterday. Dispatched by messenger, of course. No one can be more queenly than a young lady who's had a sudden smashing success. The letter contained a check for ten thousand dollars. Apparently you told Andrea of the franchise system my company uses, and apparently Andrea felt you wanted a franchise but couldn't afford one."

Barbara was touched, then offended, then puzzled. "She's difficult to figure out, sir. All of a sudden, that is. I never had such trouble in the old days."

"Their paths diverge, each has a different life's experience, so the rapport between sisters undergoes a change. Perfectly natural. At any rate, there were a *couple* of lines in the letter which alarmed me. I got the notion, don't ask me why, that this is rather like conscience money. A generous gift made to atone for something or other — you understand?"

"I think so."

"Have you quarreled?"

"No, sir."

"Are you about to?"

"No, sir. I may boot her off my houseboat one of these days, but I won't quarrel with her."

"And how does Peter figure in all this?"

The question caught Barbara by surprise.

"It should be evident to you," Mr. Nock said, "that my son is — well, fond of you. You certainly know that neither Mrs. Nock nor I would be unhappy if you chose to accept Peter's proposal. Candidly, I like you very much. You don't have Andrea's froth, but she doesn't have your substance. For the long haul, substance is what counts."

"Sir, I — "

"I know, I know." He held a hand up. "Even Peter agrees it's a one-sided romance at the moment. I must say that I approve of the way Peter hangs on, though. I myself had a long chase before I brought Mrs. Nock to the altar."

Barbara had to smile.

"Well, what do I do about the check?" Mr. Nock asked. "If you want to buy your own franchise, terms can be arranged. Actually, you could buy the franchise in a few years with the increased profits my line will bring you. I'm not especially generous in business matters, but I would be so in this case if only because I would like to see a Nock sign hanging over one of the sidewalks of Sather. In other words, I won't insist upon the customary franchise payment in advance."

"That's generous of you, sir. I was planning to make the payment, but it would've depleted my bank account.

I'd rather keep some of the money and spend the rest on store alterations. I'd like to have a river road entrance. I think my business would be increased."

"So what about the check?"

Barbara thought it over, trying to see the gift in terms of sisterly generosity. It was difficult for her to see Andy now, though, as a generous sister. Andy had returned to Sather a harder and more worldly person than before, a person not likely to do anyone a kindness unless there was something in it for her. Certainly Andy had proved that over and over again ever since Simon Levine and Abner Wallace and Mark Banes had come to town. Andy had received Simon and Mr. Wallace once. Andy had refused flatly to see Mark Banes.

"Simon's in Wallace's vest pocket," Andy had said. "Simon wants a connection at Grapnis Studios."

And of Mark Banes, Andy had said: "I want him to die for a while, Britches. There's only one way for a star to hold her own with an arrogant, know-nothing director. That's to let him die for a while."

As for the ladies and gentlemen of the *I Found A Daisy* company who'd been left unemployed suddenly? "Why," Andy had said, "in this profession, Britches, it's everyone for himself. Not a one of them, mind, said a word to defend me that ghastly evening. My understudy was actually smiling throughout Mark's tirade. I suspect she's glum now."

No, Barbara thought, the check hadn't been sent by a sister who wanted to give a girl a helping hand.

"I'll return the check to Andy," she volunteered. "I'd rather develop my own business in my own way with my own money."

He gave her the check, looking relieved, as mother and son came out to Marble Terrace. They dined at a wrought-iron table so close to the playing fountains they could feel the stirring of the cool, moist air. The Nock butler himself supervised the serving by two maids. Perhaps noticing that she was somewhat awed by the lushness of the setting and the rest, Peter began to clown around, saying he was very happy to be invited to a meal now and then so that he could see how the other half lived. His comments made the dinner downright fun. They all began to laugh, and then Mr. Nock said, "Let me tell you about the other half, young fellow. I had no training in law or anything else when I was your age. I beat my legs to death in New York City, trying to sell from door to door. The first Nock sign that went out over a sidewalk went out in the Harlem section of New York — on St. Nicholas Avenue — in the days when an elevated-train structure darkened the street. Don't you criticize me for the way I live now. I earned it. That is, your mother and I earned every stone of this place."

"But because I run my own office and live in my own hut, you complain!"

"Hang it, a father and mother do

work for their children, you know."

Peter looked at Barbara and said, "Tell them to be nice guys and let me have the sport of doing for myself what they did for themselves."

Barbara said, struck by a thought: "It *is* sport, you know, Mr. Nock. With great trepidation, you open a store or an office. You wonder if anyone will come in. You lie awake nights trying to figure out a way to improve your income. And all that's a challenge, fun."

"Two dear dimwits," Mrs. Nock tensed. And dessert having been served and consumed, she rose and reached for her husband's hand. "Leave them alone," she counseled. "The cure for this sort of thinking is a canoe ride or something."

It was a canoe ride. Peter led her to the Nock pier and helped her into a canoe while an attendant held the darned thing steady. As Peter paddled the boat upstream toward the river, the attendant lighted a couple of flares so that Peter could locate the pier should they return late. The canoe bumped and lurched when they reached river water, and then, exquisitely, the canoe began to glide. They went out a quarter of a mile to a great patch of flame and gold water. Puffing, Peter shipped the paddle and turned carefully to face her. "Far enough?" he asked. "I like to drift."

"I like to drift, too," Barbara admitted. She gazed west at the sunset, wondering why it had to be Peter there before her. Not that he wasn't a catch. In his way, Peter was probably the catch of catches in Sather. But Hugh Robards had been in her thoughts too long. Being with Peter was oddly like being with no one.

As if he'd sensed the thought, Peter said: "I grow on you. Sooner or later, all women perceive my sterling qualities."

He did have sterling qualities, Barbara recalled. For instance, he'd agreed to help Charles for nothing — or for practically nothing of value to her.

"I have a speech to make," Peter said. "You're a nice woman, Barbara. You know I want to marry you. But I think, to be honest, that my first wish for you is happiness. Understood?"

Touched, Barbara had to look away at the sunset again. The sun was dropping fast now. In just a few minutes it would be gone, and then the afterglow would come, and the darkness. She gazed around looking for a star. She saw one, but didn't make a wish.

"First of all," Peter said, "forget me for a while. Leave me out of it entirely. This thing with Hugh isn't any good. I get around town, I hear things, I observe things. It isn't any good."

"I once thought of telling Carol Robards that you can't apply logic in an emotional situation, Peter."

"That's true, provided you're an entirely emotional person. You're not. Do you know what I think Hugh is? I think he's a habit."

"Habit or not — "

"Did Andy ever tell you why she didn't marry him when she could have done so quite easily?"

"Her career."

"Nonsense. At the time, she had no career."

Peter Jay Nock said softly, "She wanted me, Barbara. Not the individual, you understand, but the Nock security."

Barbara swung her head around fast.

"I have to tell you," Peter said, "that Andy's not really interested in Hugh now. Oh, it amuses her to play up to him, to find she has the old hold over him. But she's not here for Hugh, believe me."

"Then — "

"The point is," Peter said, "that you're blaming Andy for the thing Hugh's doing. Why? Do you think we male animals are so helpless we can be enticed, just like that, against our will? Or does it soothe your ego to blame Andy for Hugh's off again, on again attitude toward romance and marriage?"

Barbara gulped air; she had to.

"A fellow can care enough for you to wake you up, even though doing so hurts him," Peter said. "I'm constantly surprised by this habit I have of working against my own interests."

And that was true, too, Barbara thought, feeling just a bit sorry for him. She fought off the urge to tell him to take her home. After all, she thought, it had been a nice dinner, and Peter was a nice fellow, and it would be a fine, fine evening, with stars blazing in the heavens and in the water.

"May I paddle?" Barbara Holman asked. "Glory, but it's coming on a grand evening!"

11

IT occurred to Andrea Lawrence as she walked the oyster-shell road inland from Sather Creek toward the crab cannery that possibly she'd been unwise to return to the Eastern Shore. An agitation among a flock of red-winged blackbirds in the roadside reeds distracted her a few moments; but after the birds had settled their difference, she returned to the gloomy thought. What she ought to have done, she decided, was buy a train ticket to Montreal and put up at the Windsor Hotel on Dominion Square. Montreal was a charming city, just English enough to be quaint and just French enough to be exhilarating. She might have made a trip along the St. Lawrence River to Quebec. She might have done many interesting things she couldn't do here. And, naturally, she'd not have felt the pull of this earth she was walking, this odd craving both for the satisfactions of her career and the rich fullness of Eastern Shore existence.

"I fear, milady," Andrea said aloud to herself, "that you're a mite confused."

A jog in the road carried her around a small yellow frame house that stood in picturesque dilapidation toward the rear of a quite spectacular rose garden. As she'd done often in other days, Andrea went to the weathered fence and rested her arms on its smooth top and called hopefully: "Anybody home? It's Andy."

An old police dog came into view on the porch and barked hoarsely. Stiffly, very slowly, the dog came down the stoop and along the path composed of earth and rectangular cement insets. Her soft, laughing, "Well, well, well, Mister," was recognized. The dog whined, as if its memory of her and its youth and the happy times they'd had together was making it ache with nostalgia. Andrea unlatched the gate and stepped into the yard. The dog came to her, one end whining and licking, the other end wagging. Andy crouched and put her arms around its shaggy neck and kissed its forehead. "There's a good Mister," she crooned. "Such a fine, fine Mister!"

Mr. Harmon came outdoors at last, leaning on a cane, smiling broadly and shaking his massive head. "About time you remembered your friends," he reproved her. "We'd have come to welcome you, but we're neither of us as young as we were. We thank you for sparing us the effort."

"Things pile up on one, Mr. Harmon, you know?"

When she'd come up on the porch, he kissed her forehead gently. He offered her a chair, then sat at the head of the stoop sideways. "It's a peculiar habit of things to pile up on one," he observed. "One survives, however. We go through cycles, I believe. For a time, everything goes well. Then the cycle changes, and everything goes less well. I often think that life would be less interesting if the changes never occurred."

The view from the porch was interesting. Beyond the fence lay a great sweep of marshland that teemed with birds. Then, off in the distance, barely visible through the tall reeds and wild grasses, lay a blue strip of the Sather River. Over the river, this day, hung great white clouds, each of which reared up to a fantastic height. The clouds appeared to be stationary, but every once in a while the sun was darkened, and against the sun Andy could see that the clouds were moving quite rapidly in an upper altitude wind.

"I bought a copy of your last book," Andy told him. "I could be wrong, I suppose, but I don't think you've ever written finer poetry. At a party not too long ago, I read six of your river songs, and everyone was enchanted."

"The singer, not the song," he said promptly. "The book does well, however. It may even earn for me the enormous sum of a thousand dollars. Being a Negro in this age of awakened social conscience does have its advantages, you see."

"It's unfortunate, Mr. Harmon, that you never wrote novels. A professor I met at the party I mentioned told me that once upon a time poetry was as popular in this country as novels are today."

"The novel never interested me, I'm afraid. Its form is loose; it's — well, you don't want a lecture on that."

"How's Lucy, sir?"

"Fine. She'll graduate next year. She talks now of wanting to do postgraduate work, but her parents think she ought to find a job."

"Nonsense. This same professor I was telling you of told me that a person ought to get at least his master's degree before he undertakes to become a teacher. I'll arrange for my bank to send her the usual check for however long it takes her to get that degree."

His black face went still as death,

as it always did when he was deeply moved. Andy reached out and gave his shoulder a little swat. "Friends are friends," she said quietly. "If one's luckier than another — well, that's what friends are for."

He asked worriedly, "What's wrong with you, Andy? I could always tell when something was wrong with you. Now Barbara, she was always different. To me, Barbara was always a sturdy live oak, and you were a young willow. I could never read Barbara as easily as I read you."

For the first time in several years, Andy was honest with herself. "I don't know what's wrong," she said. "I — well, the success isn't what I thought it would be — not at all. Now there's a peculiar thing, Mr. Harmon. When I was a child here, my ambition and my dreams rather separated me from the others. I didn't care. Things would be different; I'd have a real life, I thought, when I was a Broadway star. Yet I'm still outside, as it were, looking in."

"Why didn't you marry Hugh?"

"It would've been a form of artistic death, or so I believed at the time. I wanted to be much more than the wife of a boat builder. It made my blood run cold, absolutely cold, when I thought of the inevitable children and the inevitable pattern my life would have followed after I married Hugh. Crazy or not, Mr. Harmon, I don't think people are born to relive the lives of their parents."

"About being alone — any artist feels lonely at times."

"Darn it, sir," Andy asked passionately, "what have *you* gotten out of all the striving?"

He smiled, tugging at an earlobe. "You won't laugh?"

"God, no!"

"Well, out of all the striving I've gotten a few lines I'm proud to have written."

"And that's enough? Look at this place; look at your position in the community — and I'm not referring to the segregation either. How can it be enough?"

"Well, as Shakespeare once observed in a different context, the play's the thing."

Andy said greedily, her eyes blazing, "I want more, so much more. I want everything! I'm hungry for everything!"

His brow wrinkled. He said, "The French have a saying that each man must sooner or later effect a compromise with life. It's a fact that it must be done, incidentally. We don't make the terms of life; we're the victims, if you will, of life's terms."

"Not quite," Andy argued. "Once upon a time I was a little girl who'd come here and play with your granddaughter and Mister. You'd serve us lemonade. And sometimes you'd make up nonsense poems for us. And I was poor and bare-legged and uneducated, and I was a nothing in a little corner of America most people have never heard of. But I dreamed and I studied and I worked, and I forced life to give me what I wanted on my terms."

"That's why you're so happy now?"

Andy bit her nether lip to keep from crying. "The difficulty is," she said, "that conflict changes a person. To get ahead you must be hard, ruthless, even dishonest at times. All of a sudden you've become what you had to be in order to get ahead."

He surprised her by saying, "You can't hurt your sister, if that's what you fear. She's a live oak. A live oak stands up to the weather, regardless of storm and gale, and a live oak stands and stands and stands."

"If she ends up hating me, sir, what have I?"

"You should have married Hugh."

"I know, I know, I know. Do you think I don't know?"

"A year or so later you'd have divorced him, and then there'd be no troubling questions now."

"*Divorced* him?"

"Certainly. It takes a heap of loving

to live with a man every day, to clean his house, cook his food, raise his children, nurse him when he's ill. Now many women can do that, all that, without subordinating themselves in any way. They find completion in doing that, in fulfilling what is, after all, a rather necessary destiny. But you? Possessed of your ego? Possessed of your ambition? Yes, you'd have divorced him by now."

Andy said, "Will you not be glum? I abhor glum people. Why must people always be glum?"

And she was Andrea Lawrence the actress now, retreated from the reality of life into a role she'd trained herself to play most automatically. "I assure you," she said firmly, "that once I've undertaken something, I do it regardless of obstacles or consequences."

He did say something that reached the core of her, though, and gave her food for thought. Mr. Harmon said: "What type of man is it, I wonder, who loves this sister one day and the other sister the next day?"

Unable to answer because the question somewhat shook her, Andy murmured several polite inanities and continued on through the Negro quarter of Sather. The quarter revolted her, although it happened to be a pleasant community of well-kept houses and yards, with each street lined prettily with silver birch trees. What revolted her was the compulsion these people were under to live in this quarter of town if they wanted to live and work and raise their children in Sather. The compulsion to do anything you didn't want to do was a horrid thing, she thought furiously. Here, as elsewhere in the North or in the deepest South, change was long overdue.

She came at last to the Sather Inn. No one paid attention to her as she stepped into the cool, shadowed lobby. While she stood adjusting her eyes to darker surroundings, however, she was noticed by the man she'd charitably agreed to see despite her hatred of him. Her smile was soft, deceptively pleasant, as she allowed Mark Banes to kiss her hand. "Nice to see you on the Eastern Shore," she told him. "Having fun?"

His face craggy, his eyes bloodshot, he smiled sourly. "It's an interesting corner of America," he said. "One senses history all about one. May I treat you to lunch?"

"A Coke will do."

He took her into the Marine Room anyway. The place not being busy, they got a window table without a wait. He ordered a Coke for her and a beer for himself. He said nothing, just sat staring at the view, until after the beverages had been brought. Then: "I've talked to Simon Levine and Abner Wallace," he reported. "They contend that the production company doesn't have you under exclusive contract. They're right, to a degree. I've had several top lawyers on this, and they've made an interesting report. We do have first call on your services; primary call, in fact. If we call and you don't respond, then anything else you undertake can be considered financially damaging to us. Consequently, we could sue to recover our financial losses."

"And you would sue, of course."

"I would be very happy to sue, believe me. I would consider it a privilege to sue."

"Mark, you must never be bitter. Bitterness leads to ulcers."

"But having a runaway star does not? Interesting."

"Your public remarks inclined me to believe I was discharged. If the court orders me to return to the cast, I'll do so."

"Nice of you. Now let me tell you something, Andrea. I intend to spend at least the next five years of my life smashing you as you smashed *I Found A Daisy*."

"Why must this be a personal quarrel?"

"Very simple explanation. I needed a smash hit. I had four flops in a row on Broadway and three flops out in Hollywood. Everyone was yammering I'd lost my touch. Then I take a relative unknown and develop the smash musical of the season. And what happens? The star quits and does her best to damage my professional reputation."

His eyes troubled her. They had about as much compassion in them as you'd expect to find in the eyes of a reptile.

"You didn't call me here to threaten me, I'm sure," Andy said. "What did you want to propose?"

"You're wrong," Mark Banes said. "The play is closed, the cast broken up, the lease on the theater gone. There's nothing left for you to return to, Andrea, not a thing. So if I can do it, I'll see to it that your career's left as you left *I Found A Daisy*."

"But Bruce said — "

"You guessed wrong and he guessed wrong. The backers and I know a valuable property when we have one,

Andrea. You were both wrong to think that we'd sell out to Bruce after you'd killed the thing by walking out. We unloaded the package on Hollywood for four million dollars. With the stipulation, of course, that Miss Andrea Lawrence, the great and beautiful Daisy, could never play in the movies the role she created on the stage."

Andy went ashen.

"You won't love Jane Creach's columns next week," Mark predicted. "I gave the full story to her."

While Andy sat there utterly speechless, Mark Banes finished his beer and walked out.

12

LIKE just about everyone else in Sather the last week of May, Barbara Holman read Jane Creach's syndicated column with lively interest. She did so at the store, not wanting to offend Andy by reading the work of a woman whom Andy viciously called, 'A jackal seeking to feed on carrion.' It seemed to Barbara that Miss Creach had done considerable research before she'd undertaken to write the series of columns under the general title: *The Strange Case of Andrea Lawrence*. For example, Miss Creach began her first column with a quite touching allusion to the long-term friendship of Andy and 'the great Negro poet, Alton Harmon.' She quoted Andy as having once said: 'Anything I know about art and artistic integrity, I learned from Mr. Harmon.' And there were other little touches here and there all week long to indicate that Miss Creach had done an honest job of trying to get to the heart of Andy's character before she'd written a line. Former high school chums and acquaintances of Andy's had been interviewed. People she'd worked for in Sather had been interviewed. And the New York interviews! Certainly Miss Creach had striven to be fair. Yet despite the fairness, the portrait of Andy that gradually emerged was both shocking and frightening. Worse, Barbara thought loyally, the portrait bore little resemblance to Andy. It was almost as if Miss Creach had mixed up notes she'd made about Andy with notes on some other celebrity.

At the end of the week, Barbara went to Hugh's boat yard with all the clippings and half an apple pie. She caught Hugh in his office at the far end of the corrugated metal building in which the finishing touches were given to the smaller sailing craft he manufactured. Her appearance without notice of any kind took Hugh by surprise, as she'd hoped it would. Easily, amiably, Barbara stepped in and laid the pie on the desk and confided, "I thought we might have a little chat before we scandalize everyone in the country. Do I return your ring, or would you rather I stand waiting in vain on the steps of the church?"

He did flush, she had to give him credit for that. Also, he did look somewhat like a man who rather wished at the moment that he'd not been born. He had in his make-up, however, a certain quick-mindedness that served him well now. "Nice of you to bring the pie," he said. "I've been meaning to have a talk, but I've been busy."

Barbara took the chair near the window. The office was as cluttered and untidy as ever. The desk, heaped with all sorts of papers, was a downright disgrace. "How do you keep an eye on your business?" she had to ask. "I should think you'd never find the papers you need."

"Oh, I make out," he commented. "Each person has his own system, that's all. Look, I'm not proud of myself, Barbara. One reason I've avoided seeing you is that I'm pretty ashamed of myself."

"Why be ashamed?"

"Well, a man my age ought to know his own mind, that's for sure. And Andy won't ever be a tenth the person you are, and a man's stupid and even crazy to look into those big blue eyes and let them hook him for a second. But those are just words, Barbara. All I know is that when I came aboard the *River Lark* that first evening and saw Andy there — well, I came alive again."

Barbara swallowed hard and forced a broader smile.

"Now get this," Hugh said. "I intend to marry you. Not this June, as we planned, but when Andy's gotten her affairs in order and has gone back to New York. I'm not entirely nuts, you know. I know better than you or anyone else that Andy and I wouldn't stay married a year. But right now — "

"Why would you marry me, Hugh?"

He met her large, patient, good-humored eyes. He cupped his face in his hands, then dropped his hands to his lap. "It's all so crazy," he said hoarsely. "Who is she; what does she do to a guy?"

"I don't know," Barbara said unhappily. "I wish right now I did know. I think I do know why you'd marry me after she's gone, Hugh. A person has to have something, isn't that it? If he can't have the sun, he'll accept the moon, and if he can't have the sparkle he'll at least take the home. Isn't that it?"

"It's more, you know that."

"If there were more, Hugh, we'd marry as planned and invite Andy to the wedding."

Out in the big building, a thump sounded, and then Carol called: "Hugh, are you here?"

Barbara asked quickly, "Yes or no, Hugh? I have to be told."

"Look, she has enough grief right now, Andy has. I can't hurt her any more, you know that."

Which was, Barbara decided, an honest answer of a kind. Surprised by her calmness, she removed her engagement ring and laid it on the desk beside the pie. "You may want this for Andy," she said. "It's a quite nice diamond, I'm told."

"Look!"

Barbara rose, grinning, as Carol stepped into the office. "No," she told Hugh. "I'm really not that desperate, you see."

Chunky Carol stopped short, her gray eyes flashing. "Hugh," she scolded, "this is a junk yard, not a business office. Look at that desk! Look at the — "

Carol saw the ring. Carol stopped talking, her mouth agape.

Barbara went with what she hoped was proper dignity to the door. She was halfway through the big building before both the Robards called out, but of course she just quickened her steps. The impact of it all didn't hit her until just as she was leaving the boat yard. When it did hit her, she stopped short. She looked around hotly, wildly, so furious for a moment that she wanted to screech, to claw. Somehow, though, she clung to her self-control. She went quickly back to the main part of town. She went directly to the Sather Inn and had the clerk tell Simon Levine that she wanted to see him in a big hurry. Simon came downstairs in shirtsleeves, a rare thing for him. "If it's about your sister," he said, "forget it. If it's about you, here's an ear."

They went to the Marine Room again, and he brought her dinner. "You should be Andy," he said wistfully. "You're a nice, quiet, sensible, beautiful kid. Why weren't you Andy?"

"No talent, I'm afraid. Andy gets the talent from her father, I'm afraid.

According to Mom, Mr. Lawrence was a talented man."

"What happened to him? I never heard."

"Korea happened to him, Mr. Levine. Mom came here and Mom stayed here."

"I see. Rough."

"It wasn't the Korean war, in case you misunderstand. Mr. Lawrence was a newspaper cartoonist. He made a trip to Korea and liked it so well he decided to stay there. He never called his act abandonment of wife and child — he called it fulfilling his artistic destiny."

Mr. Levine's eyes widened. "She got the scattiness from him, too, is that it?"

"It isn't scattiness, Mr. Levine, in my opinion. It's just that Andy emphasizes things we don't emphasize."

"Like ganging up with a sharpshooter to make a great big kill? Personally, I believe Jane's stories, Barbara. It figures. Bruce Hogan's known in New York for fast work to make a kill. Andy's been influenced by that character in more ways than one. A sweet plot! Walk out of a smash hit, buy up the wreckage, then make the wreckage a smash hit again."

"Can such things be done?"

"Anything can be done, Barbara, if the timing is right, if other factors are present. For instance, the folks who produced *I Found A Daisy* did it on a shoestring. Why do you think Andy got the lead? If they'd had money to work with, they'd have bought an established star. I suspect that Bruce Hogan figured they'd pant to sell once they felt the economic pinch of Andy's walkout. Luckily for the producers, though, Andy made it a really smash thing, and Hollywood saw and Hollywood grabbed."

Barbara asked practically: "Where does all this leave Andy, Mr. Levine?"

"Up the creek."

"Oh?"

"I'll listen to her when I've calmed down, of course. But if the words are wrong, she doesn't even have an agent. You can be sure that Grapnis wouldn't touch her then with a hundred-foot pole. If she doesn't marry Hogan or one of the other rich guys who dated her in New York — well, I'd guess she'll be right back where she was before she ever came to New York."

"Even though she's so talented?"

"Talent's not so rare, Barbara. Also, a producer will settle for less talent and more dependability any old day of the week. Why not? A lot of money is put into a show or a movie. You can't take chances with undependable talent when big money's involved."

"Still — "

But that was when Peter Jay Nock strode in, obviously looking for them. Peter sat between them and announced: "Andy wants me to sue Miss Creach and the syndicate that distributes the columns. She'll not accept less than ten million dollars, should they want to settle out of court."

Simon Levine carefully laid his knife

and fork just so across his plate. He said in hushed tones: "A nice sum of money."

"Well, she's a bit annoyed with Miss Creach and the syndicate," Peter explained. "Mr. Abner Wallace sent her a letter stating that any interest he may have expressed in employing her has undergone a change."

"If they'd hired her, she'd have gotten twenty-six thousand over a thirteen-week period," the agent said. "That isn't ten million."

"What's a star's potential, Mr. Levine?"

"How can anybody say?"

"Have any stars earned ten million, sir?"

"More than one, sure. But — "

"Here's a young beautiful star, Mr. Levine. According to the New York critics — and Andy showed me the columns — she's the freshest, most exciting young star to come along in years. One critic predicted she might well become the box-office draw of the century both on Broadway and in motion pictures."

"Well, they deal in superlatives, you know."

"In your opinion, sir, it's utterly impossible she could have achieved that stature?"

Simon Levine scowled. "Look," he said, "in show business nothing's impossible. But — "

"But what, sir?"

Simon asked, looking confused: "Do you mean to sit there and suggest she has a chance?"

Peter said coolly: "I sent the syndicate and Miss Creach a wire yesterday, sir, announcing our intention to sue unless the libelous material were withdrawn and a full apology made. No answer. Today's column appeared. So we sue."

Aghast, Barbara cried: "But who has ten million, Peter. Good heavens!"

Simon Levine excused himself promptly. After he'd gone, Peter grinned. "Now there's a fellow who's going into a mental huddle with himself," he said, "to figure out what to do next. What do you think he'll do next?"

"Stick with Andy, as he always has. Advise her to forget this nonsense, to patch things up in New York, to get on with her career."

"What do you think Andy should do?"

"What I've just said."

"I hate to tell you this," Peter said, "but Andy's now decided she wants ten million dollars and Mr. Hugh Robards."

"Hugh and I aren't engaged, by the way."

Peter began to smile — and stopped.

"What do you think Andy should do?" Barbara asked.

"See a psychiatrist."

After a long time, Barbara confessed: "I've been thinking that, too."

Simon Levine returned, brisk and self-assured once more. There was, interestingly, a happy gleam in his fine dark eyes.

13

ON what was to have been her wedding day, Barbara went early to her store to watch the new sign go onto the iron brackets over the red brick sidewalk. She considered it an historic occasion, and after she'd opened up and made her customary checks of the counters and racks, she settled down behind her desk and gave thought to putting on a combination open house and sale to celebrate the event. The district superintendent of the Nock chain arrived a few minutes later to snap a photo of the sign and to have her sign the necessary papers. He looked the store over and nodded approbation. "You have a nice beginning," he said. "Of course, if your experience is typical of other Nock merchants, sooner or later you'll have to give thought to expansion. Do you own this building, or what?"

"According to my father, Mr. Dystrup, no one owns anything until the last mortgage payment's been made. I do have the mortgage though."

"The whole building?"

"Yes, sir."

"The shoe store next door — have they a long lease, or what?"

"Two-year lease."

"Then you're in an excellent position, Miss Holman. How old are you?"

"Almost twenty-five."

"Good. Right now, the nature of your arrangement with us considered, you have a substantial debt. But you're young enough for time to work for you, and you have a good location in a growing community. Next year I'll assign one of our experts to analyze your entire operation. Frankly, it's my belief, based on the experience of other Nock affiliates, that our line will improve your net income the first year by approximately five thousand dollars. It might be to your advantage to pay off your mortgage with the extra income. Then you could take over the adjoining shop for the inevitable expansion."

Barbara had to laugh. "You mustn't make me a great success so quickly, sir. I'm the sister who has to plod through life and earn everything the hard way."

She signed the papers and offered him a cup of coffee. He accepted the offer, a stocky, moon-faced man in his middle age. "Speaking of your sister," he said, "it might be an excellent idea for you to take her into a limited partnership. According to Mr. Nock, she might be a ready source of capital. Let me tell you something about business, if I may. It's no trick to make money if you carry a good line of quality merchandise and if you work at your business as you should. What gets most small businesses into trouble is lack of adequate capital. All that merchandise is, basically, is money converted into stock and placed on a counter for sale. A Nock toaster is really just eight dollars laid on a shelf until someone comes along to give you fifteen dollars for it. The more stock you have, the greater your potential."

"These are all established prices, sir?"

"Very much so, Miss Holman. We do considerable research before we price an article. Comparison shopping is done, quality comparisons are made — and so on. Our records show that Nock merchandise is entirely acceptable to the general public at the prices we establish. We never approve of cut prices. You'll find in your copy of our agreement, in fact, a clause that forbids you to cut prices without written permission."

"What about an opening sale, sir?"

"We've thought of that, naturally. We think it poor psychology, however, to introduce a line by cutting prices one day and returning them to normal the next. What we do, therefore, is provide our new affiliates with a cash allowance for coffee and sandwiches and souvenirs. We pay for announcement advertisements in your local newspapers. And we contribute three door prizes without cost to you: a color television set, a power lawn mower, and a top-quality sewing machine."

Barbara stared.

"Such attractive door prizes," he said, "do attract attention, we find."

A truck came rolling to a halt before the store. A few minutes later, the truck crew and Mr. Dystrup had taken over the store. The television set, the lawn mower, and the sewing machine were mounted on special platforms set in one of the windows. Gaudy signs were pasted across the three show windows. Next, ladders were brought in, and the men strung banners to and fro near the ceiling. By this time, of course, all the activity had attracted a good crowd of curious people, and soon the curious were coming inside to look over the few Nock things that had already been placed on the counters. Much to her delight, Barbara was able to sell a Nock toaster to a woman while Mr. Dystrup was standing nearby. He grinned as the woman walked away. "Now your eight dollars has become fifteen dollars," he said. "Care to try for a hundred?"

Thanks to Mr. Dystrup and all the excitement, the June day passed swiftly and quite pleasantly. At least two hundred persons came into the store for a look around. A few disapproved of all the changes, but most seemed to be pleased by the establishment of the Nock line in the community. Many looked, but quite a few bought, so that by the time Tad Ott arrived after school, there was a real need for his strong arms and quick legs. Tad quickly replaced the sold merchandise and then saw to the coffee making and serving. The next thing Barbara knew, Tad was also functioning as ticket giver-outer and salesman. Amused, Barbara watched him in action whenever she could, thinking that possibly he could teach her a few things about selling to the teen-age set. But she noticed presently that, although Tad greeted the teenagers quite pleasantly, most of them came to her for service, and few of them so much as nodded to Tad before they went on out. During a lull, she asked Tad if he'd offended his girl or something. Tad startled her by saying tautly, "They let Charles Snively out of Juvenile Hall, Miss Holman, and all the kids think I should quit so he can get his job back."

"I didn't know he'd been released."

"At school today I heard all kinds of chatter, Miss Holman. Most folks think that Mr. Snively took all the blame, that he said he'd forced Charles to go poaching with him."

Barbara telephoned Mrs. Snively at once. She had a long, long wait, and when Mrs. Snively answered she sounded cross and tired. She perked up somewhat when she recognized Barbara's cheery, "Hi, there, Mrs. Snively. May I speak with Charles?"

"Miss Holman," Mrs. Snively said, "I won't never forget that you hired

Mr. Nock when everybody else was dead against 'em."

"Well, Charles and I are friends, you know. I'd like to chat with him."

"He's out on the river, Miss Holman. Men and boys — you'd think they'd get some sense, wouldn't you? He gets into trouble on the river, so the minute he gets home, he goes out on the river."

"He still has a job with me, Mrs. Snively, if he's at all interested. Will you tell him so?"

"Miss Holman," Mrs. Snively said, "I honest to God think you're a real lady."

Embarrassed, Barbara contrived to end the conversation as soon as she decently could. She had Tad come to her office directly after they'd closed. She waved him to a chair and told him the decision she'd made about Charles. Just as his face began to freeze up, she asked Tad how he'd like to be one of the youngest sales clerks in Sather. The China blue eyes came alive again. "I was sort of hoping to be a sales clerk next year," Tad said. "You sure you think I'll be okay this year?"

"I'm sure you'll make the customary goofs and exasperate me on occasion and even annoy a few customers, Tad. On the other hand, you're bright, alert, interested. I think it will be an excellent arrangement for both of us. I'll have a bit more free time, and you'll have a larger income. Suppose I pay you a dollar and a quarter an hour until school vacation comes along? I'll need you full time during the summer, of course, and I'll start you out at fifty dollars and raise you if you deserve a raise."

"What about Charles?" Tad asked. "A guy could get jealous."

"Charles isn't interested in a career in retailing. I'm sure he doesn't want a full-time job, either."

"Would I boss Charles?"

"Boss him? Why?"

"Well, suppose you go out, leaving us here alone. Suppose he goes over near the cash register. Can I tell him to turn his shoes around and walk somewhere else?"

"I don't see why you should, Tad. Charles was perfectly honest in his dealings with me."

"I sure wouldn't want to be able to get into the cash register if he can too. Look. Miss Holman, Charles never did have a clean rep at school. Nobody ever caught him at anything, but nobody trusted him, either."

"Well, I'm different," Barbara said composedly. "I trust everyone until I have just cause not to."

A knock sounded on the door. It was Mr. Leroy Nock himself, of all people, come to admire the sign and to look over the premises. He came into the store, all but exuding a boy's satisfaction. "Kid stuff or not," he said, "that sign gave me a thrill, Barbara. How was business today?"

"Quite good, sir. Your Mr. Dystrup gave me some useful business tips, too."

"Dystrup's a competent man. You listen to him. Merchandising is a science to Dystrup. He collects every scrap of information he can from the retailers; he analyzes, he correlates, he broods. When he tells you to do this rather than that, he has a good reason for doing so."

Barbara beckoned Tad over and introduced him to Mr. Nock. "My new sales clerk," she added. "Tad yearns for a career in retailing."

"Whatever I am," Mr. Nock declared, "I owe to the fact I once had the same yearning, son. You stick it out and learn all you can. In this country, it's the salesman who's king. Until somebody sells a product, no one gets paid."

He led Barbara out to his limousine. "I'm to dine with you," he announced. "Peter and his mother have gone to New York looking for ten million dollars or so. Peter thought you shouldn't be alone to brood this evening."

"I did my crying and brooding, sir, last week."

"Robards is an idiot."

Barbara settled down in the passenger compartment as the chauffeur eased the limousine smoothly from the curb.

"You know," Mr. Nock said, "a young woman could do worse than accept Peter."

"Much worse, sir."

He met her tranquil brown eyes and sighed. "The trouble is," Mr. Nock said, "that women your age are always too emotional."

14

TOO emotional or otherwise, Barbara thought in the moonlight on the *River Lark*, she'd not planned and dreamed just to lose Mr. Hugh Robards by default. Maybe Hugh wasn't perfect. Maybe he'd always been drawn toward Andy. Maybe she herself was the idiot. Still, she'd come this far through life entirely satisfied Hugh was the fellow she wanted to marry, and she knew darned well she'd always have the same longing regardless of anything that happened. So —

A footfall behind her interrupted the thoughts. Andy, lovely in a filmy negligee, was standing near the salon door, watching her. A scent of violet came to Barbara's nostrils. A sound of deep breathing came to Barbara's ears. Suspecting an apology in the offing,

Barbara said quickly, a bit curtly, "Go back to bed, Andy. It's been a long day for me, and I'm not in the mood for conversation."

"The moonlight's lovely, isn't it? I was watching it stream through my window. How delightful it would be if one could catch the moonlight in a glass and — "

"And have it to enjoy when you're back in New York? I'll send you a glassful."

Andy asked, surprised: "You're inviting me to leave?"

"No. Let's just say I think you'd be wise to return to New York before Mr. Bruce Hogan learns about you and Hugh."

"Why ever should I please Bruce?"

"Andy, Peter and I had quite a discussion about you and your career and your lawsuit. The key figure in the lawsuit is Mr. Hogan, naturally. Suppose he becomes so angry with you he testifies in a manner favorable to Miss Creach and the newspaper syndicate?"

"Darling, you've lived in Sather too long. A man such as Bruce may do many things, but he never does a personally damaging thing. And, really, there's little he can say. It may surprise you to know this, but Bruce and I didn't gang up on the producers for the reason Miss Creach gave. In fact, we didn't gang up on anyone, period."

"I think, though, that your place is in New York."

Andy came to the rail and stood with her hands resting lightly on the rope. She said flatly, "It would make no difference to Hugh and me, Britches. Whatever you want, though."

"You actually think Hugh would abandon his business to live in New York with you?"

"I didn't know I was planning to live in New York. Britches, Britches, Britches, you seem to know so little about me or my affairs. I've made money, Britches. I have a nice income from the record album I cut when

I Found A Daisy became a smash. Also, Bruce has invested my money quite shrewdly. We've even been partners in several profitable real estate ventures. Hugh and I could live quite comfortably here in Sather even if I never worked again."

"But — "

"Naturally," Andy said, chuckling, "I don't expect to win any ten million dollars. I do think, however, I have a good chance of being awarded several hundred thousand dollars."

"I can't believe," Barbara said, "that Miss Creach would make a goof like that."

"Barbara?"

"Andy?"

"You mustn't hate me, dear. You see, I've always loved you deeply."

"I won't ever hate you."

"You have to understand, you see, that life goes by so rapidly. At the back of your mind, you plan to do this or that after you've accomplished this or that. You think there's so much time.

Then, suddenly, you realize that others are living their lives and that you don't have as much time as you thought. Do you understand me?"

"I think so. You received a letter detailing my agreement to marry Hugh in June. You suddenly realized that if you didn't act quickly, you'd lose Hugh. You also suddenly realized that you didn't want to lose Hugh."

"Frankly," Andy said, "I have as much right to be angry with you as you have to be angry with me. Hugh and I were always sweethearts. But the moment I left, you gave Hugh your full attention."

"You did leave," Barbara reminded her.

"Not to pursue another man, though, but to pursue a career at a time when Hugh really wasn't able to afford marriage. There's a difference."

"When do you marry?" Barbara asked.

"The important question, Britches, is what happens after Hugh and I are married. To you and me, I mean."

"Nothing melodramtic, Andy. I'm not the type for melodrama."

"We smile and kiss in sisterly fashion when we meet, but we meet seldom?"

"If that often."

"But if it were the other way around, you'd expect me to be a good sport?"

Barbara thought that they'd be arguing bitterly and vehemently in another minute. She said abruptly, "I'm tired, Andy. This day has been — well, difficult."

Andy asked coldly, "Shall I leave now or in the morning?"

"Whenever it's most convenient, Andy, will be soon enough for me. You might spend a few days with our parents. You've not been thoughtful in that respect, you know."

"I won't be scolded!"

Wryly amused, Barbara went to her stateroom and settled down in her big double bed.

The Bruce Hogan thing came back into her mind. She gave it thought until she fell asleep, and the next day she wrote Bruce. Andy was gone when she got back to the house-boat, and so was the deputy Constable Allard had put on guard duty at the catwalk entrance. Several kids were swimming joyously quite near the *River Lark*, and several other kids were having a cookout on her scrap of private beach. Barbara was invited to eat with them, but before she could accept Hugh came driving up in his pickup truck. Hugh boarded the *River Lark* and settled in a deck chair in the stern. "What's with you and Andy?" he asked. "I had to come here this afternoon for her luggage."

"Well, you know me, Hugh. One reason I live here is that I enjoy peace and quiet. Also, I did think she should spend some time with the folks."

"She's talking of buying the Pruett farm."

"Really? Well, that ought to be convenient for you."

"That's a nasty crack, Barbara. I told you in my office that I'm not crazy. I told you I planned to marry you, not Andy. I'm getting tired of hints that I'm planning to do something I'm not planning to do."

Barbara took a chair, feeling the need of support sturdier than her legs happened to be at the moment.

"For your information," Hugh said, "I'm not the sort of man who goes around marrying women because women do big things to me. First of all, I'm an adult. I know as well as you that it's a long-term deal, a lifetime deal, the sort of deal you don't make with just anyone. Do you want to hear more? I know that if I broke a leg and couldn't work for a year, I couldn't count on Andy for support. I could count on her seeing me through a cold if the cold hung on a week. She isn't the type."

"I didn't know that men married women to pick up a form of guaranteed nursing service, Hugh."

He balled his hands into fists. "Sometimes," he said tensely, "you make me angry. That was a mean crack."

"If we married tomorrow or so, the nursing service would be available forthwith."

He jumped up. "Look," he asked, "do you want me to leave? Are you kicking me overboard, too?"

"I really didn't kick Andy overboard."

"And I'll tell you something more while we're on the subject," Hugh grated out. "I'm sick and tired of being looked at by everybody in town as if I'd mistreated you. I don't know what you've been telling people, but I haven't mistreated you. My big mistake was being honest with you."

"Hugh, I'd reather not quarrel."

"For your information," Hugh Robards snapped, "Andy's having a rough time. She could easily lose everything she's worked so hard to get. Read the newspapers! All right! So once upon a time Andy and I were sweethearts. She's still drawn toward me, just as I'm drawn toward her. If she was up there on Cloud Nine right now, I wouldn't care if I hurt her by marrying you while she's in town. But she's not on Cloud Nine, and I don't want to hurt her."

"Suppose she left tomorrow?"

"What are you trying to do, Barbara — nail me down to an iron-clad contract?"

Her laughter offended him. He did leave, so red-faced and so sputteringly angry that the kids in the water and on the beach looked at him wonderingly.

Next, the telephone rang, Hollywood, it seemed, wished to talk with Miss Andrea Lawrence. Barbara announced coolly that Andy wasn't there, and a man's voice asked somewhat tensely where Andy could be reached. Barbara recognized Mr. Wallace's voice. "I couldn't say," she told him. "When I hear from Andy, I'll have her call you, Mr. Wallace."

"How did she react to my letter, Miss Holman?"

"She wasn't happy about it."

"The trouble is," he complained, "that directors can't always make the big decisions. After the Creach columns, the vote out there went against your sister. I've been working to make people realize she's as much sinned against as sinning."

"Have you succeeded, sir?" Barbara asked.

"To a degree, Miss Holman. If your sister were to fly here and submit a properly humble request for employment, Mr. Grapnis might accord her three or four seconds of his time."

"*The* Mr. Patrick Grapnis, sir?"

"The great man, Miss Holman, for whom I'm privileged to work."

"But nothing's changed here," Barbara warned the director. "Andy simply refuses to shift an inch from her contention that she was in effect discharged."

"That's another matter, Miss Holman. May I give your sister the considered advice of a rat? Sooner or later, an actress has to act. If she doesn't act, she's just another doll in a world overcrowded with dolls."

"There would be a job this time?"

"Naturally, only Mr. Grapnis can make these decisions. No one else can speak for Mr. Grapnis. It's possible sometimes to guess what he'll decide, and I think I've guessed the answer to the big question, or I hope I have."

"Wonderful, sir."

Humming as she hung up, Barbara changed her mind about the character of Mr. Abner Wallace. She waited a few moments, then telephoned her mother and gave her the message to pass along to Andy. Her mother said dubiously, "I don't think she'll be interested dear. She's quite upset about you."

"About time."

"Barbara, please don't give me any trouble. I have one scatty daughter too many as things are."

"Has Bruce Hogan telephoned her, Mom? I gave him your number."

"Yes."

"I don't suppose you'd care to tell me what was said?"

"Very little was said, dear. Andy listened, murmured a few words, and said goodbye to him. It must have been unpleasant, however. Andy was pale when she hung up."

"I'd guess, Mom, that he told her she won't be getting ten million dollars from anyone."

"Barbara?"

"Mom?"

"Hugh isn't the first boy in history who met an old flame and found himself warming up a second time."

"I know."

"Then?"

"But I won't be married," Barbara said sharply, passionately, "because the fellow thinks I may make a dependable nurse in an emergency."

Eyes flashing, Barbara stopped talking, figuring she'd said all that needed to be said on the subject to her mother and anyone else who might be interested.

15

IN his lush, air-conditioned office on the hot July morning, Abner Wallace contemplated the slim, beautiful blonde woman he hoped to transform into a personal meal ticket for five or six years, "Not to complain, Miss Lawrence," he said, "but you took your own sweet time about making up your mind. I telephoned back in early June. A lot of things can happen out here in five weeks."

"I adore your office, Mr. Wallace. I abhor settings."

"Well, I grant you it isn't bad, not bad at all. I did want a desk topped with pink marble, but my shows were slipping when I made the request, and the request was ignored."

"Here and now, Mr. Wallace, I promise you shall have a marble-topped desk. I firmly believe that people should have what they want."

Abner Wallace busied himself with the intercom. Very patiently, if slowly, he worked his way up through the echelons whose primary function in life seemed to be to guard the great man's time as if each second of it were a diamond. The top woman said at last that she would probably call him back in a few minutes. Abner settled back in his chair for a long wait. Ten seconds later he was told to escort Miss Lawrence into the presence. Flushing, beginning to perspire, Abner got Miss Lawrence upstairs to the large, quiet office with the stained glass windows. Mr. Grapnis rose and bowed and seated Miss Lawrence personally. "A distinct honor to have you here, Miss Lawrence," he said. "So few have genuine beauty and talent."

The smile of the woman, Abner saw, could be magic when she wished it to be. His scalp tingled. Sitting down, he decided she might be his personal meal ticket for ten years, at least. Such a beautiful woman should surely make it big in motion pictures as well as in television.

"This lawsuit" — Mr. Grapnis said — "I don't like it, Miss Lawrence. If you knife the press in the belly, the press will return to the attack. In the long run, it's better never to knife the press in the belly."

Andy said, "If I worked for your organization, Mr. Grapnis, I would of course be guided by your wisdom in these matters."

"So!"

"Sir," Andy went on, "I really have been libeled by Miss Creach. The fact is that I endured a great deal for the sake of the show. When I could endure no more, I left."

"So!"

"And there was an emotional problem, sir. Am I less a woman because God has blessed me with this great talent? I don't think so. My emotions don't feel so. But none of this had anything to do with my decision to accept my discharge without protest."

"So!"

"My trouble has always been, sir, that I've lacked a steadying hand during times of emergency. There are some things a woman can't tell her male agent. And then — "

"It pleased me to discuss your career with your Simon Levine, Miss Lawrence. I like the man. He has an honesty I admire. For instance, he told me that at the present time your career, to be crude, is up the creek."

"Yes, sir."

His black eyes sharpened. "I wonder why you don't argue this?" he asked. "I have to be fair, Miss Lawrence, and warn you never to come to Grapnis without any weapons in your hand. I'm a very hard man to cope with when I have the advantages."

The blue eyes danced, and those eyes, Abner saw, also worked a certain magic.

Andy said simply, "I must throw myself upon your mercy, sir, it would seem. I find this odd. Still, there it is."

"So!"

Mr. Grapnis swiveled his chair about and sat contemplating St. George and the dragon's head. He said presently, "I made a little deal yesterday, Miss Lawrence. I went to a man who had a product I wanted, and I said I'd pay him four million dollars for it in cash. So I bought a thing called *I Found A Daisy*. Then I telephoned some people in New York. Those people said I could milk the product for a couple of years on Broadway, easy, if I had you in the leading role."

"Yes, sir."

"Then I telephoned a man named Mark Banes and told him he could have a big dramatic series to direct for me next year if he took that stinko clause out of the contract he made with the studio that bought the musical. The stinko clause forebade anyone from putting you in the part."

"Yes, sir."

"Miss Lawrence, let me be frank with you. I can get the original cast together, and I can get that musical back on Broadway by August first. After all, August is a dull month in New York. You can always find a theater, and you can always rehire actors and actresses who've been starving in hall bedrooms."

"Yes, sir."

"I like your humble spirit, Miss Lawrence. Even if I didn't like it, though, I'd give you a break. I'm always a sweet guy to people who throw themselves on my mercy. Ask Abner Wallace."

"Sir," Abner said, "I sincerely admire your generous nature."

"You're very kind, sir," Andy said

"I'll give you a package," Mr. Grapnis announced. "I'll give you the lead in *I Found A Daisy*; I'll give you the lead in Abner's *Turtle Bay*; I'll give you the lead in the movie version of *I Found A Daisy*. As I'm sure you can see, it's a five-year package, at least."

"Sir, I'm almost speechless!"

"Five thousand a week for five years — right across the board, Miss Lawrence."

"Oh, dear! Mr. Levine thinks I should have ten."

"Miss Lawrence, are you suddenly losing your humbleness?"

"Sir, I'm under contract to Mr. Levine. If he tells me to work for a dollar a week, I'll do so."

"So we'll make it eight. Who's quibbling? Don't answer yes or no. I'll iron out the details with Levine."

Andy rose promptly. "I feel," she said, her voice exquisitely musical, "that I'm working for a top organization, sir. May I thank you for the honor?"

Mr. Grapnis smiled modestly and accompanied her to the elevator . . .

* * *

In Bruce Hogan's office, several days later, Andy signed the contract assuring her of four hundred thousand dollars a year for the next five years. Simon Levine took the fountain pen reverentially from her hand and wrapped it up in a scrap of Kleenex he bummed from her. "I want to save this fountain pen," Simon said. "This is an historic occasion."

"What's money?" Andy asked.

Bruce said brusquely: "If you start that malarkey with me again, Andy, I'll break your nose. Money's what everyone tries to get and few people succeed in getting."

Bruce nodded to his secretary, and the woman went out and brought Jane Creach inside. The newspaper woman looked around a bit apprehensively. "Listen, folks," she said. "I'm simply a little girl who's trying to make her way in the great big world. I'm not authorized to make a deal with anyone. Is that clear? I'm here to listen to a proposition, period."

"Jane," Bruce growled, "you and your syndicate have been after me a long time. That's okay. I'm a big boy who can look after himself. But Andy's different. Andy's a small-town girl who lacks our experience and resourcefulness."

Miss Creach asked, laughing, "I wonder who's kidding whom."

"Now what we're doing," Bruce growled on, "is letting you and your syndicate off the hook insofar as money is concerned. To get anywhere with that lawsuit will take Andy years, and she can't sit it out waiting, because the public forgets too darned soon."

"Very sensible," Jane Creach said promptly. "You want a retraction, I take it."

"Right."

"No, sir."

They were all startled.

Jane turned to Andy and said, "I got the entire story from Hugh Robards, Miss Andrea Lawrence. You sat bragging to him aboard the *River Lark* one day. Bit by bit, I got the story from him."

"Preposterous," Andy sputtered.

"Miss Lawrence, I guarantee you that Mr. Robards will be called as a witness for the defense. In view of your mutual infatuation, I don't think anyone will consider him a witness unfriendly to you."

Andy said huskily, "You wouldn't dare!"

"I have my professional reputation to protect, Miss Lawrence. I'd have to dare."

"Jane," Bruce said, "a guy who's loved and lost is apt to tell quite a few lies to anybody who'll listen. Andy's going to marry me. Robards is the guy left out in the cold. Do you think the jury or judge will believe he isn't trying to get even?"

"Just the same — "

"Here's what you do," Simon Levine said in a kindly tone. "In the first paragraph of your column, you apologize to Miss Lawrence. In the next five or six paragraphs, you explain to the readers that at last you've been able to determine that a hitherto trusted source gave you a bum steer. Then you wind up the column by announcing this package deal Andy's made to appear again in *I Found A Daisy* on Broadway and then in the movies. And then — "

"Whoa," Jane said, "where's the telephone!"

"The big thing to emphasize," Simon Levine said, "is that I've wangled four hundred thousand a year for the next five years for this young and beautiful star."

Bruce Hogan coughed huskily.

"Or maybe," Simon said, "you'd better mention that Miss Andrea Lawrence has become engaged to marry Mr. Bruce Hogan. A lot of people prefer to read about sloppy romance."

* * *

Feeling tired, at peace, and tremendously rich, Andy stretched out on the chaise longue on her bedroom terrace in the cool of the foggy New York evening.

Nowhere on earth could she see New Jersey. The river! Where, oh, where, was her lovely Hudson River? Sighing, Andy rang the little handbell for Mrs. Rennick. When the woman came out, Andy said: "I'll have an omelette and a bottle of seltzer, Mrs. Rennick. Have they moved New Jersey in my absence?"

"It's the fog, Miss Lawrence. May I offer you some roast pork?"

"You're a dear creature, Mrs. Rennick, but you may not offer roast pork."

"You eat too little."

"Will you not be glum?"

"Still — "

"We may be commuting frequently the next few years between New York and Hollywood, Mrs. Rennick. I do hope you adore flying."

"Ma'am, what you've gone and done is make a fabulous deal, just fabulous. When I read the paper, I was that proud of you. Aren't you glad you came home from the Eastern Shore? Big things never happen in tank towns, and I should know."

"And if I say to you, Mrs. Rennick, that a fragment of my heart lies permanently buried on the Eastern Shore?"

"No, Miss Lawrence."

"But I have a sister, you see, a remarkably lovely and amiable and stupid sister. I could hardly have her marry a low character, could I? Regardless of what you may hear to the contrary, Mrs. Rennick, always believe that I went to Maryland not to get the man for myself but to spare my sister the grief of marriage to him."

"Whatever you say, Miss Lawrence."

Andy wet her lovely lips, finding it difficult to go on. But on she went, speaking softly, tensely, her blue eyes bulging in their sockets. "I'll reward you for your devotion, of course, Mrs. Rennick. At any time you could have told Miss Creach exactly what you overheard Mr. Hogan propose to me one evening in the living room. You held your tongue. You did me a service. I can be kind and generous, Mrs. Rennick; never think otherwise."

"To me, Miss Lawrence, you've always been. Take that young Negress at college. Why shouldn't I be loyal to you?"

"We came close, Mrs. Rennick. We came very close to getting full control of that marvelous musical. But who'd have expected Mark Banes to close a deal with a studio? We never expected that."

"Such things happen, Miss Lawrence."

"Oh, well," Andy consoled herself, "four hundred thousand a year spends well."

The fog lifted! There, strikingly, were the Hudson River and New Jersey!

16

THE newspaper stories concerning Andy caused tongues to wag in Sather. Mr. and Mrs. Nock found it interesting that a little girl on whom they'd once spent a little money had in a short time reached the eminence of four hundred thousand dollars a year. "You know," Mr. Nock told Barbara almost reverently, "that's a lot of money. Even if most of it does go to the Federal government in the form of taxes, it's still a lot of money. I was almost fifty before I was earning half that amount each year."

"Andy once told me, sir, that a person in show business has to make big money in a hurry. She said that the public's so fickle. She mentioned a lot of old-time stars who don't have a dime today, even though they earned fantastic salaries at a time when taxes were negligible."

Peter came out of the house, carrying a box of cigars for his father. Peter set the box on the wrought-iron table, hesitated, then took a cigar for himself. He lit up thoughtfully, brow furrowed, eyes brooding. With half his face obscured by smoke, Peter said, "I'd like to know more about the story behind those newspaper stories. Oddly enough, I've gotten no instructions to call off the lawsuit."

"Miss Creach did apologize, though, Peter," Barbara pointed out. "I thought she did it rather cleverly, too. Among other things, Miss Creach said that she was so happy to have read in the newspaper headlines that she'd *not* damaged Andy's career. Miss Creach said she was sure other stars would pay her to write blasting columns about them if they'd end up as Andy had."

"But what would Andy be earning right now," Peter countered, "if Miss Creach's blasts hadn't put Andy in a bad bargaining position?"

"Who'll know?" Mr. Nock said. "Son, don't ever be a quibbler. Just sock Andy with a big bill for your services and go on to your next case."

Peter let the matter drop for the time being. Barbara and he challenged his parents to a game of croquet and were soundly trounced for their youthful cockiness. After ice cream under the Japanese lanterns, Peter invited himself to walk Barbara home through Sather to the houseboat moored in Sather Creek. They took the winding river road. There was a moon when they reach Town Park, so of course Peter said they ought to sit a while on one of the benches, and they did. Barbara waited for the inevitable arm to go around her shoulders. She'd be polite, she decided. A hug wouldn't break a girl, nor would a kiss or two. And who could say that when she was an old lady, grateful for a quiet corner to creep into, she'd not look back through the years to this particular moonlit July night and remember happily that a fellow had found her fair, worthy of being hugged and kissed?

"Were you afraid?" Peter Jay Nock asked.

"Afraid?"

"Sometimes, Barbara, the friend of a client talks to a lawyer by long-distance telephone. The telephone rings, an operator says it's New York calling, and then a man's voice growls: 'Nock, this is Bruce Hogan — I've gotten the screwiest letter from Andy's kid sister.' So, Barbara, I repeat the question: were you afraid?"

"Of what?"

"That Andy would marry Hugh?"

"Nonsense."

"Well, why did you write the letter?"

The moonlight struck beautiful gleams from the river. Close in, a fish rose to the moonlight and dimpled the water. Now the gleams ran everywhere in ever-widening ripples. If you dove into a moonlit ring of water, Barbara remembered, a wish would come true. So Andy had once told her . . .

"I was afraid," she conceded, turning to look at Peter's moonlit face. "But not that Andy would marry Hugh."

"What were you afraid of?"

"Peter, it was a goof for Andy to come here. Sure, it was a quiet corner to creep into. But she forgot that a kid sister learns quite a bit about an older sister over the years. After Miss Creach wrote that so-called libelous series of columns, I asked the inevitable questions. And had a convincing tale of innocence to tell. But she hasn't been able to fib successfully to me in years. Whenever Andy's telling a fib, she lifts her left hand awkwardly and pulls at her left earlobe with her thumb and middle finger. She's done that for years."

"I see."

"So I was afraid, yes. I happen to adore Andy, I happen to admire Andy, I happen to respect Andy. How could I let her do such a thing? I knew darned well that even if she did get the blasted ten million dollars, she'd despise herself the rest of her life. Andy's not greedy for money; she's never been that. She's just greedy for fame, for all the attention that's given a star."

"A lot of people become greedy for money if they have even a dream of snagging ten million dollars."

"What did Mr. Hogan tell you?"

"What you hoped he'd say to Andy, I suspect. He said he hadn't given Andy an antique brooch just to lose her to a tank-town boat builder. He ranted on that way for five minutes or so, and then he growled that he was lowering the boom on Andy. What happened after that is anyone's guess."

Now a sailboat came gliding across the moonlit river. It was a yawl. Its set in the water told Barbara that it was a yawl that had been designed and fashioned by Hugh Robards. It seemed almost unreal in the moonlight, a fantasy concocted by a sleeper whose eyes were wide and staring.

Peter held his watch up so the moon

could shine on the dial. Eleven o'clock on a fair July night with a good breeze blowing from the east. "That should be Carol and Andy," Peter said casually. "Andy telephoned late this afternoon. She had a friend who was flying to Cambridge, and she asked me to have Hugh arrange for her to be picked up there. Hugh has a big job in the yard, so Carol agreed to fetch Andy in the yawl."

All of Barbara went cold.

"I have to tell you," Peter said, "that Andy's hopping mad. I suppose she wormed the real story out of Hogan."

Barbara rose quickly. "I'd better get to the *River Lark*, Peter. Thanks for the warning. Now I know why you seemed so disturbed this evening."

"I always walk a girl to her door," Peter said. "Old-fashioned of me, I suppose, but who cares?"

"If you don't mind, Peter? I abhor people who travel over two hundred miles just to squabble with their relatives."

They moved on again along the river road. For a time the yawl appeared to be ahead of them; then they appeared to be ahead of the yawl. They of course reached the houseboat long before the yawl could even turn into Sather Creek. Barbara had time to make coffee for Peter and even to check the guest stateroom in the unlikely event Andy should elect to spend the night there. She remained in the salon when Carol turned the yawl in, under power, and called for someone to throw her a line. Peter threw the line. Then Andy was aboard, chattering about the simply divine moonlight sail and what she proposed to do to her sister's eyes if she could get her nails into them. Grinning, Barbara sat on the couch as Andy came in through the starboard door. For perhaps the first time in her life she beat Andy to the punch. Coldly, she said, "Oh, it's you. I thought it might be Betty. Why is it you? I abhor glum people. A crook is always glum, haven't you ever noticed?"

Andy said hoarsely, "You traitor!"

"I'm sorry, Andy, but you're not welcome aboard the *River Lark*. Do you leave, or do I telephone Constable Allard?"

"I dare you! I dare you!"

Barbara reached promptly for the telephone. "First, Constable Allard. Second, the editor of our little newspaper. Please, sir, would you like to know why Barbara Holman just had the police drag her very own sister off the *River Lark*?"

"I *dared* you! Go ahead!"

Barbara dialed the number and waited for Constable Allard to answer. When he answered sleepily, she said, "This is Barbara Holman, Norm. I'm sorry to wake you, but Andy's aboard my houseboat, and she won't leave, and I want you to make her leave."

"Barbara, is that sisterly?"

"I'm sorry, Norm, but if you don't come, I'll have to wake up the president of the Town Council."

Barbara pronged the handset. She waited a few moments, then began to dial the home telephone number of the newspaper editor who'd once told her he couldn't ignore a big story. Mr. Keyes also answered sleepily. He came awake fast, though, when Barbara had given him the story. "Let me get my camera," he begged. "My God, let me get my camera."

Barbara pronged the handset again. She smiled at Andy. "You have perhaps five minutes, at the most."

"Darling, hasn't anyone told you that an actress is a good judge of acting? You mustn't play-act for my benefit."

Peter came in and sat on the arm of the big chair near the door. He said to Andy, "Miss Lawrence, perhaps I ought to say, as your lawyer, that all this is ill advised."

"She turned me in! She actually turned me in to Bruce!"

"I'd do it again," Barbara said cheerfully. "I abhor crooks, you see."

Andy sat, so furious she couldn't speak.

"I know," Barbara said. "You think I've given you a poor return for all you've done for me. Who gave me this houseboat? Andy. Who loaned me a thousand dollars so I could open a little store? Andy. See? I know all you've come here to remind me of. And because I did remember and because I did feel grateful, I wrote that letter to Bruce Hogan."

"Of course," Andy said sarcastically, "Hugh had nothing to do with any of it?"

"Not really."

"So that if I tell you I've returned the antique brooch to Bruce, you won't feel perturbed?"

"Not really."

"Let me tell you why I'm here, darling. I wanted to tell you that as of this moment, this very second, we're not sisters any more. I'll never forgive you for betraying me, not ever. And now I'll tell you the rest. It occurred to me on my bedroom terrace that it's quite possible for a woman to have a career and also the husband of her choice. Life's easy, very easy, for a woman earning four hundred thousand a year. You see? So I telephoned Hugh, and he agreed that life with such a woman would be quite agreeable for him, too."

Peter said, "You have about three more minutes, Miss Lawrence. I just heard the siren."

Andy snapped: "By the way, Mr. Nock, you're discharged."

Peter smiled. "Oh, in that case, Miss Lawrence, stick around for as long as you wish."

Andy got up, muttering, and went to the starboard door. She stood there for ten or fifteen seconds; then she whirled and asked Barbara: "Don't you understand? I'm not acting now. I'm not."

The siren came shrieking to the waterfront. A spotlight lanced through the night, centered on the catwalk, and was held fixed there. Constable Norm Allard came fussing and fuming along the catwalk, both hands on the rails. He invaded the salon in the manner of a man who wanted to paddle the britches of two young ladies he'd happened to watch grow up. "Andy," he said, "I'm ashamed of you. Look what time it is — almost midnight, and you making trouble like this."

"I defy you to arrest me, Norm."

"Who wants to arrest you? Just get off this houseboat so I can go home and get some sleep."

Andy turned to Barbara. "That's how it is, then?"

"Yes."

"I won't ever see you again."

"You've already said that."

Now another car came through the night. Andy gasped. It seemed for a moment that Andy would blow sky high with fury. But before Mr. Keyes could come aboard and snap a sensational picture for a sensational news story,

Andy zipped out the port door of the salon and hustled aboard the Robards yawl.

Barbara, recalling she was hostess, got coffee for her three male visitors.

17

VINCENT HOLMAN said, "Barbara, we have to talk." He came aboard the *River Lark* in the sweetness of early morning, his lunch pail banging against a knee, the legs of his overalls flapping in the sunrise breeze. He sat in a chair facing the Robards Boat Yard. After she'd brought coffee to him, he said, "I hate to see the old firms go out of business, don't you? A lot of history was made in that boat yard. Four generations of Robards worked there. Did you know that?"

"Yes." Barbara gazed at the boat yard for a time and then decided to make things easy for her father. "Hugh went back to New York with Andy, I suppose?" she asked.

"Yeah."

"Carol won't operate the yard?"

"Right now, I can't think that's important."

"But it is. As you said, a lot of history was made there. Also, if the yard is closed, what happens to men who've worked all their lives there?"

"I guess the Robards don't care."

"I guess not. Nor Andy."

Vincent Holman said sturdily: "Sure she cares. Now look. Maybe Andy approaches things different, but she's no monster. It's just that she cares in a different way. Without any publicity, she helps a lot of folks."

"Dad, could you operate the boat yard?"

A peculiar expression came over his face. "Look," he said, "you don't seem to understand. Hugh went to New York to marry Andy."

"Well, I should *hope* so, Dad. The last thing Andy can use right now is a scandal."

He set his coffee cup on the desk. "I don't get it," he said hoarsely. "Andy comes to the house last night all blubbery because you washed her out of your life on account of Hugh. Then I come here to break the bad news to you, and you stand there smiling."

"Why not? If she cares that much about Hugh, the marriage will last. It's pleasant to know that, don't you think?"

"But — "

"Dad, I returned Hugh's ring. He was as sweet as any man could be in the circumstances. He even said that after Andy had gone back to New York, he'd marry me. But it was so — well, I did return the ring, you see."

"Then if you felt that way — "

"Dad, I'm not an arch enemy of Andy, after all. All right. I did resent her coming here and doing what she did. I was furious, in fact. But when you get right down to it, what else could she do for her man? She walked away from the smash musical of the year and came close to losing her career. She invaded her own sister's home to act like a sneak. She — well, what else could she *do*?"

"When you put it that way," Vincent Holman said, "even I want to spank her."

"Well, she did have another reason for walking out on that musical. What difference does it make? The fact is, they were all happy to get her back. Another fact is that Hugh was happy to get another chance at Andy. So like a good little girl, I'll send them a present one of these years. And who knows? Perhaps when I meet them in my old age, I'll be able to laugh and pretend I never really did care."

"Hey."

Just why the tears came then, Barbara Holman never knew. She was quite surprised by them. She'd thought she'd gotten all the tears out of her ducts forever during the long hours after she'd returned Hugh's ring. What was there to cry about now? She had this houseboat, growing business, her family, her friends. Why, she even had the love of Mr. Peter Jay Nock. And just wouldn't it stun Andy if Andy knew that some day Peter Jay Nock would inherit a fifty-million-dollar retail empire!

Presently the tears stopped. Barbara was able to suggest to her father that he go to work. After he'd left, she had her customary fifteen-minute swim in Sather Creek and then cooked herself a hearty breakfast. At eight o'clock sharp, she headed for the store, feeling not a bit tired after all the excitement, feeling not a bit depressed by the realization that at almost twenty-five she was still a single girl with no serious romantic interest in her life. She stopped on Leggett Point to watch some fishing boats head off on the long trip to Chesapeake Bay. In the Negro section of Sather, she stopped to admire Mr. Harmon's rose garden. The old gentleman called a greeting from the porch and came with his dog to the gate. "All well with Andy?" he asked. "She's not written me lately."

"Right as rain, Mr. Harmon. She really did sign that fantastic contract, and now she's being married."

"Oh?"

"Hugh Robards, sir. Isn't that nice?"

"Hugh? How odd. In her letters she chattered ad nauseam about a Bruce Hogan."

"Well, women have the privilege of changing their minds, sir. And men, too, I understand."

Who knew what he was thinking? The face showed nothing; the eyes looked far, far away. Then he said, "Did I ever tell you, Barbara, that I have a pictorial concept of people? To me, for example, Andy has always been a flame raging out of control. To me, for example, you've always been a charming, sturdy little wake-robin growing in some quiet place. Isn't that interesting?"

"I like to think, sir, that Andy now has what she's always wanted. How's Lucy?"

"Fine. She sent me some fudge. Why

don't you stop in some evening and have a piece?"

"You're kind, sir."

"Naturally. I've always had the privilege, you see, of the friendship of two kind ladies."

Touched, feeling oddly humbled, Barbara walked on through the streets of her home town, nodding to this one, waving to that one, stopping now to chat, now to listen, now to laugh. Mr. Keyes called to her as she passed the doorway of his office. He came out into the sunshine and stood there blinking sleepily. "What happened last night?" he asked. "I have the feeling I missed a big story."

"Sorry about that, sir. I'll make it up to you one of these years."

"No need for that. Stories happen or they don't happen; a man either gets them or he doesn't. Did you hear the rumor about Hugh Robards?"

"Which rumor, sir?"

"Oh, some idiot told some idiot that Hugh Robards went to New York to marry Andrea Lawrence."

"Really?"

"Well, you know how it is with even middle-aged reporters, Barbara. We check out even the rumors passed along by idiots to idiots. Hugh said there was no truth to the rumor at all."

Barbara's heart seemed to miss a beat.

"What did happen, Hugh told me, Barbara, is that some woman old enough to know better tried to turn the clock backward too many years. But he said to her, or so he told me, that it was a new day, a new year, and that he liked the present much better than he'd ever liked the past."

Barbara said huskily, "Sir, you'd not fool a girl, would you?"

Mr. Keyes said a bit stiffly, "Newspaper reporters report the facts and only the facts, Barbara, as I've told you before." He started to go into his office, then turned. "I thought I saw Hugh waiting for you to open your store, Barbara. I could be wrong, I suppose, but I never am."

Now, moving slowly, every step a delicious ache, Barbara went on up the street and across the road and up still another street to where a certain red brick sidewalk began. Charles Snively was hosing the sidewalk with a fine spray, using the spray as he would a broom to sweep leaves and sand out to the gutter. Charles switched off the spray to avoid wetting her shoes and stockings. He gave her a happy smile. "Tad said," he told her, "that him and I can handle things be you gone some. Tad sells 'em, and I take the cash money."

"Do you mean," Barbara teased, "that Tad now trusts you?"

Charles shrugged. "Could've stole from you all the times I was alone in the store. Dumb fool Tad never thought of that until I tongued him."

Charles pointed along the parking lot. Barbara went through the parking lot to the rear. Charles had already begun the fence dismantling so that the construction crew could transform the back of the store into an attractive entrance and display setup. Hugh was in the yard, looking over the plantings. He grinned when he saw her. "The Sather Garden Club won't love you for tearing up these gardens, you know. One of the ladies gave Charles a bad time yesterday."

"Mr. Nock gave me a good idea on that subject, Hugh. He suggested that after the renovation's completed, I offer the garden club a hundred dollars to work out a landscape design for me. I think I'll do just that. These women are my friends and neighbors and potential customers, after all."

It occurred to Barbara that he looked thin and drawn and dreadfully tired. She sat in a shady place on the grass and gestured for him to join her. "When did Andy leave?" she asked. "It was around midnight when she left me."

"Oh, about three in the morning.

I have quite a fine sister, you know. Carol dislikes sailing at night, but she sailed Andy back to Cambridge and her friend with the airplane."

Barbara had to ask: "Are you sure, Hugh? It's a long life, I should think, if you're not sure."

"What about you? I left you in the lurch. How do you know I won't do it again?"

"The first time, it was Andy's decision not to marry you. This time — well, apparently it was your decision. There's a difference wouldn't you say?"

"Your father thought it was time I stopped bugging you. He said he could prove to me it was all over, that you didn't care."

"Sometimes fathers know less than they think they know. How did Andy take it?"

"I don't think she believed it for a while. Then she was upset. I'll tell you something, Barbara. I won't be the last man to feel her pull. There's a magnetism you can't understand unless you're a man. Maybe that's why she's big on Broadway. I guess the fellows in the audience feel that pull over the footlights."

"But?"

"That was quite a letter you wrote Bruce. After he read it to me on the telephone — a fellow doesn't deserve you, Barbara. There I was, apparently playing the heartless fool. There you were, humiliating yourself to a tough cookie for the likes of me."

Blushing, Barbara said, "He shouldn't have read it to you. All I wanted was to get him stirred up. Andy told me such a preposterous yarn about her antique brooch — as if a man would give such a thing to a girl unless he planned to marry her."

"It was a no-sweat decision after all," Hugh said. "I thought of how it's always been between us when Andy wasn't here: the houseboat and the store and the boat yard, the town and our friends and this way of life.

So Andy came and talked, and then I told her that today is always better than yesterday. She was offended, her pride was hurt, she did some crying. About three minutes later, though, she was the same cocky Andy she's always been, talking about the reopening of the play, talking about her television series, bragging about the elegant mansion she'd have in Beverly Hills. I got the feeling that Andy considered me a darn fool."

"And I suppose that Peter and his folks are thinking the same thing about me."

Hugh said soberly, "That's a lot of importance you're refusing, Barbara."

"I've always been sentimental, not practical, I'm afraid."

He looked at her sitting there with her face turned to the river, a grave face, a lovely face, a face with strength in it but with gentleness in it, too. The cheek nearest him attracted his lips. After the kiss, she swung her eyes to him and said, "It'll be all right with

Andy and Peter, I'm sure. Andy didn't come for you, not really. Not to offend you, but she was alone on the boat a good deal and quite disturbed. You came, and she remembered the old days . . . Peter? He always knew I'd never let you go."

A kingfisher came along, just skimming over the broad and beautiful Sather River. The bird was Andy, Barbara thought, wild and free. Then thought stopped, for Hugh was putting the engagement ring back onto her finger. He had difficulty. "Maybe you don't want it?" he asked. But she worked her knuckle, and the ring slid on. It looked grand on her finger, Barbara decided. It felt *right*. This time, excited, she let his lips find her lips.

Other titles in the Linford Romance Library:

A YOUNG MAN'S FANCY
Nancy Bell

Six people get together for reasons of their own, and the result is one of misunderstanding, suspicion and mounting tension.

THE WISDOM OF LOVE
Janey Blair

Barbie meets Louis and receives flattering proposals, but her reawakened affection for Jonah develops into an overwhelming passion.

MIRAGE IN THE MOONLIGHT
Mandy Brown

En route to an island to be secretary to a multi-millionaire, Heather's stubborn loyalty to her former flatmate plunges her into a grim hazard.

WITH SOMEBODY ELSE
Theresa Charles

Rosamond sets off for Cornwall with Hugo to meet his family, blissfully unaware of the shocks in store for her.

A SUMMER FOR STRANGERS
Claire Hamilton

Because she had lost her job, her flat and she had no money, Tabitha agreed to pose as Adam's future wife although she believed the scheme to be deceitful and cruel.

VILLA OF SINGING WATER
Angela Petron

The disquieting incidents that occurred at the Vatican and the Colosseum did not trouble Jan at first, but then they became increasingly unpleasant and alarming.

DOCTOR NAPIER'S NURSE
Pauline Ash

When cousins Midge and Derry are entered as probationer nurses on the same day but at different hospitals they agree to exchange identities.

A GIRL LIKE JULIE
Louise Ellis

Caroline absolutely adored Hugh Barrington, but then Julie Crane came into their lives. Julie was the kind of girl who attracts men without even trying.

COUNTRY DOCTOR
Paula Lindsay

When Evan Richmond bought a practice in a remote country village he did not realise that a casual encounter would lead to the loss of his heart.

ENCORE
Helga Moray

Craig and Janet realise that their true happiness lies with each other, but it is only under traumatic circumstances that they can be reunited.

NICOLETTE
Ivy Preston

When Grant Alston came back into her life, Nicolette was faced with a dilemma. Should she follow the path of duty or the path of love?

THE GOLDEN PUMA
Margaret Way

Catherine's time was spent looking after her father's Queensland farm. But what life was there without David, who wasn't interested in her?

HOSPITAL BY THE LAKE
Anne Durham

Nurse Marguerite Ingleby was always ready to become personally involved with her patients, to the despair of Brian Field, the Senior Surgical Registrar, who loved her.

VALLEY OF CONFLICT
David Farrell

Isolated in a hostel in the French Alps, Ann Russell sees her fiancé being seduced by a young girl. Then comes the avalanche that imperils their lives.

NURSE'S CHOICE
Peggy Gaddis

A proposal of marriage from the incredibly handsome and wealthy Reagan was enough to upset any girl — and Brooke Martin was no exception.

A DANGEROUS MAN
Anne Goring

Photographer Polly Burton was on safari in Mombasa when she met enigmatic Leon Hammond. But unpredictability was the name of the game where Leon was concerned.

PRECIOUS INHERITANCE
Joan Moules

Karen's new life working for an authoress took her from Sussex to a foreign airstrip and a kidnapping; to a real life adventure as gripping as any in the books she typed.

VISION OF LOVE
Grace Richmond

When Kathy takes over the rundown country kennels she finds Alec Stinton, a local vet, very helpful. But their friendship arouses bitter jealousy and a tragedy seems inevitable.

CRUSADING NURSE
Jane Converse

It was handsome Dr. Corbett who opened Nurse Susan Leighton's eyes and who set her off on a lonely crusade against some powerful enemies and a shattering struggle against the man she loved.

WILD ENCHANTMENT
Christina Green

Rowan's agreeable new boss had a dream of creating a famous perfume using her precious Silverstar, but Rowan's plans were very different.

DESERT ROMANCE
Irene Ord

Sally agrees to take her sister Pam's place as La Chartreuse the dancer, but she finds out there is more to it than dyeing her hair red and looking like her sister.

HEART OF ICE
Marie Sidney

How was January to know that not only would the warmth of the Swiss people thaw out her frozen heart, but that she too would play her part in helping someone to live again?

LUCKY IN LOVE
Margaret Wood

Companion-secretary to wealthy gambler Laura Duxford, who lived in Monaco, seemed to Melanie a fabulous job. Especially as Melanie had already lost her heart to Laura's son, Julian.

NURSE TO PRINCESS JASMINE
Lilian Woodward

Nick's surgeon brother, Tom, performs an operation on an Arabian princess, and she invites Tom, Nick and his fiancé to Omander, where a web of deceit and intrigue closes about them.

THE WAYWARD HEART
Eileen Barry

Disaster-prone Katherine's nickname was "Kate Calamity", but her boss went too far with an outrageous proposal, which because of her latest disaster, she could not refuse.

FOUR WEEKS IN WINTER
Jane Donnelly

Tessa wasn't looking forward to meeting Paul Mellor again — she had made a fool of herself over him once before. But was Orme Jared's solution to her problem likely to be the right one?

SURGERY BY THE SEA
Sheila Douglas

Medical student Meg hadn't really wanted to go and work with a G.P. on the Welsh coast although the job had its compensations. But Owen Roberts was certainly not one of them!

HEAVEN IS HIGH
Anne Hampson

The new heir to the Manor of Marbeck had been found. But it was rather unfortunate that when he arrived unexpectedly he found an uninvited guest, complete with stetson and high boots.

LOVE WILL COME
Sarah Devon

June Baker's boss was not really her idea of her ideal man, but when she went from third typist to boss's secretary overnight she began to change her mind.

ESCAPE TO ROMANCE
Kay Winchester

Oliver and Jean first met on Swale Island. They were both trying to begin their lives afresh, but neither had bargained for complications from the past.

CASTLE IN THE SUN
Cora Mayne

Emma's invalid sister, Kym, needed a warm climate, and Emma jumped at the chance of a job on a Mediterranean island. But Emma soon finds that intrigues and hazards lurk on the sunlit isle.

BEWARE OF LOVE
Kay Winchester

Carol Brampton resumes her nursing career when her family is killed in a car accident. With Dr. Patrick Farrell she begins to pick up the pieces of her life, but is bitterly hurt when insinuations are made about her to Patrick.

DARLING REBEL
Sarah Devon

When Jason Farradale's secretary met with an accident, her glamorous stand-in was quite unable to deal with one problem in particular.

THE PRICE OF PARADISE
Jane Arbor

It was a shock to Fern to meet her estranged husband on an island in the middle of the Indian Ocean, but to discover that her father had engineered it puzzled Fern. What did he hope to achieve?

DOCTOR IN PLASTER
Lisa Cooper

When Dr. Scott Sutcliffe is injured, Nurse Caroline Hurst has to cope with a very demanding private case. But when she realises her exasperating patient has stolen her heart, how can Caroline possibly stay?

A TOUCH OF HONEY
Lucy Gillen

Before she took the job as secretary to author Robert Dean, Cadie had heard how charming he was, but that wasn't her first impression at all.